T0064063

THE GOLDEN
TOUCH

THE GOLDEN TOUCH

HARI MENON

PARTRIDGE
A Penguin Random House Company

To order additional copies of this book, contact
Partridge India
000 800 10062 62
orders.india@partridgepublishing.com

www.partridgepublishing.com/india

For Extra Ordinary Love and Trust,
Love and Understanding
I dedicate this book to
Mom (Jayasree Kishore) & Dad (Vrija Kishore)
Ammini, Harish, Mahesh and Kishore
Reshmi – My better half
And to my life itself... Aarhav and Aarnav
If it is to be... It is because of them

Special Mention

Map: Anand Krishnamurthy

**There would be a few chapters in this book
that may not be suitable for all readers.
Certain chapters are violent in nature**

This book is for entertainment purpose only,
any resemblance to the living or dead is
purely coincidental. And everything, from places
to technology, is pure imagination of the writer.

Mysteries are due to secrecy.

Francis Bacon

1

B randon Brookes tall and well built with dark blue eyes with a well combed hair with a small scar on his left forehead, which he is very proud of, which he got during a war that he led as a commanding officer while he served in the Army; A story that he boasts about.

Even though he has a Masters in Paleontology, an education, he never used whiles his career in the Army. During his tenure, he picked up a new interest; interest in weapons; its make and its precision. He always wondered about its invention which actually went back to the times of the kings and queens of the olden days from cannons to today's war tanks and machine guns.

He always wanted to be a Paleontologist; call it fate or destiny, he landed up in the Army.

As is his character he didn't let go of things easily. He was determined to serve his country as faithfully as he can be, which gave him the courage to face any situation and earned him all those medals and ranks along with fame.

Now that he is retired and is leading a peaceful life in a quiet neighborhood away from everything; people he know to the people he hates. A regular visitor to his home is always his milkman early in the morning.

He enjoyed his retired life by keeping himself updated with the latest weapons with the help of magazines and internet. He also took up Gardening as a hobby, an art that he was planning to master apart from the knowledge and experience in martial arts and mathematics.

He used his spare time to develop his knowledge that he has long forgotten – Paleontology; latest discoveries, updates, latest technology, each and every detail that is happening around him.

Even though he is in his early sixties, if there is a poll for the sexiest man alive in that neighborhood, his name would lead the rest.

June 11 2011

Checked his watch after a good long run, tired he removed his custom made Bluetooth headset and was about to enter his house, he noticed a letter on his pavement addressed to him.

Only a very few knew about his address after his retirement from the Army, he was leading a very peaceful life. Away from all the people, who wants to be with him and away from those who wants him dead!

It's been a long time since he received a letter and he was not expecting one. As he was living on his retirement benefits and all the inheritance that he received, he lived a luxurious life.

With great curiosity, he took that letter, and kept it on his study table. He came back outside to water his flowers and the rest of the garden and cleaned his car, while returning all the pleasantries from the ladies next door.

He came back, took the letter from the table. His cleanliness would talk a lot about him. On the left side of the living room is a Chinese vase which is passed down the generations and is 3000 years old. A wall mounted television, a small refrigerator with all kinds of beverages. According to him, precious time can be spent with the guests talking rather than going to the kitchen to get them something to show his hospitality. The only catch was – he never had any guests. But there was no harm in being prepared.

Behind the living room is the dining room to which you need to climb at least 5 steps and the best part was the person in the living room cannot see what he is doing there. A well made dining table from maple wood and a nice glass bar cabinet filled with exquisite drinks and 25 sets of different glassware's and jars for all occasions.

Towards the ride side is a room, which he calls his work area; filled with books a nice stereo surround home theatre, video camera, his personal laptop and a desktop with all necessary applications from GPS tracking to Photoshop. You name it, he had it. To add glory to the room, he had a nice study table with lots of draws; each for a specific item that he has marked and all his draws had a digital number lock. As a very careful person; every time he punches his code some sort of liquid is sprayed on that to wipe his fingerprints off the lock. The room was filled with a television on one side of the wall and on the other side; he had an air conditioner to fit all weather conditions. The remotes were well placed on his study table along with his collection of pens and a wall cabinet with his vintage gun collection.

He kept the letter on his study table and kept a rock that is actually from the age of dinosaurs on top of the letter so that it doesn't fly away. He uses that as a paper weight even though that is a priceless piece.

He proceeded towards his bedroom, a well made bed with a beautiful view facing a small lake outside and on the other side he had his wardrobe with all expensive suits to his casual wear ironed and well kept; a dress for all occasions which was categorized and was kept ready. He had a bag packed and kept in case of an emergency he can take it and leave. The bad included a spare laptop, a phone and all necessary things that he might want during his journey.

He had a shower, made himself a nice hot chocolate and went straight to his study where he can relax and read the letter that he saw on his pavement.

2

Detective Bryne, how may I help you?

Hello, Detective, I'm Ambra Gallo.

Yes! How can I help?

I'm calling to check about my father who has been missing for the last 3 years. I've lodged a complaint then.

Well Ms. Gallo, this is the homicide and Auto theft investigation department, you should be calling the missing persons team and they should be able to throw some light on this one.

I completely understand, probably because you are new to this team you are unable to understand. As it's been more than 3 years, they moved the case to the homicide investigation team and removed the file from the missing person's database; hence I'm calling you to check on that. Some new policy it seems.

Alright! Didn't know about that, do you have anything handy, which would actually help me dig up the case details like a case reference number or something?

I don't have anything of that sort as you are the first one to ask me that. Would the name of the missing person help?

Yes! Give me the name please.

Franco Gallo. Spelt as F-R-A-N-C-O G-A-L-L-O missing since 2009 and he is my father.

She could hear the sound of the keys through the phone along with voices of laughter and other conversations going on in the background and after a while the voice came back.

I just pulled the details, but I'm sorry that I do not have any news to bring a smile to your face. I do have the update and progress of the investigation though. But I cannot share that with you as it's an ongoing investigation. Anyways, would it be possible for you to meet me at 7PM near the front gate of the stadium of Utica.

I'll be there and the line went dead.

Ambra Gallo, daughter of a wealthy industrialist Franco Gallo, who settled in the United States through generations even through their blood-line, is from Italy.

She is 5 foot 5 inches tall with straight blonde hair hanging beneath her shoulders and is always let free. She is smart and shrewd, sensitive and sensible, listens and thinks, all deadly combination and too perfect to be a lady. Her pretty spotless face and her sweet smile; she could get away with things but at this point none of those qualities are of use. As she is currently bothered about is only about her father who went missing 3 years ago who went on a holiday to see all the Seven Wonders of the World in one trip.

Franco Gallo the wealthiest industrialist, who actually started his career with his collection of extra ordinary vintage cars and bikes, which actually fetched him a good price, from that he understood that he would get buyers for vintage items. Then slowly and steadily he started to grow and his wealth started to multiply and to this day, it has not come down; the graphs were always showing an upward trend. His craze for artifacts has taken him to places that no one has dared to go. More money came to his hands through the artifacts that he sold than his car manufacturing company.

Feb 13, 2008 | JFK International Airport | American Airlines flight to Rio de Janeiro

Hello this is your captain Matt Redneck and would like to personally thank you all for choosing American

Airlines flight to Rio de Janeiro as your preferred airlines today. While we make all attempts to make your journey worthwhile and keep up to your expectations, there would be some unforeseen delays. We know that your time is valuable and let me first apologize for the inconvenience that this delay might have caused. We understand that this flight is already delayed by an hour and the reason is that one of our premier customers who have booked the flight was not able to reach on time. I just got the information that he has reached the airport and has started his boarding formalities.

Franco Gallo, as he boarded the aircraft, he went straight to the cockpit, with his dignity, reputation and power that was a walk in the park for him. He apologized for being late and he also requested whether it would be possible for him to speak to the other passengers for holding them back, a request that the pilots obliged to. The airplane started to backup and started to prepare the engine for its takeoff.

Hello, my dear fellow passengers, I Franco Gallo would like to apologize as I have kept you waiting, despite your busy schedule. I'm sorry once again. And he handed the mic back to the captain and headed to the business class where the stewardess showed him to his seat.

Ladies and Gentlemen, this is your captain. The flight Boeing 767 JFK to Rio is ready for her departure. And even though we are delayed, we would try our best to make sure that you arrive your destination on time and if the winds are favorable.

The flight backed up completely; fasten seat belts sign was switched on; the airplane taxed on the runway and now it's airborne to Rio de Janeiro.

3

Franco woke up with a jolt as the airplane came to down. He stretched himself as the announcement was going on –You are now free to use your mobile phones and other electronic gadgets, please remain seated till the seat belt sign is switched off and please do not try to remove your baggage's until we come to a complete halt. We know you have many choices for the airlines and we thank you for your patronage and we look forward to serving you in American Airlines again. And as we promised, we are here in Rio de Janeiro as scheduled.

As Franco came out of the airport there was a man waiting for him with the placard "The Marriott Hotel Welcomes Franco Gallo" with a smile he drew near him. The chauffeur quickly took the luggage from him and escorted him to the limousine which took him to the hotel.

As a regular guest of the hotel, he was welcomed by the relationship manager who has kept all the papers ready and all he had to do was sign. He passed through the form again and in the list of areas where he delivered to tick Business or Pleasure, he stroked business for the first time and ticked on pleasure and smiled. And one of the staff escorted him to the Presidential Suite. As he moved to the suite, he made a request at the reception that he would require a car and a chauffeur at all times at his disposal until he vacates; a request that they obliged to.

By the time he freshened up and came down, the car was waiting for him.

Where to, sir?

Take me to the beaches first, let me, explore the land first hand, always was here on business and never for pleasure, so throw me a treat as it's your home. The driver smiled and brought him to the Copacabana beach. The beach was filled with tourists from round the macrocosm and the situation has been jammed with all sorts of people at the Rio Carnival was about to occur during that time of the year. And he could sense the life in the gentle wind and everyone speaking around it; as they are anxiously waiting for that appointment.

After expending sometime in the sun, he came back and articulated to the Christ Redeemer please.

No sooner he came at the redeemer with the very first expression; he realized why it is on the top 7 wonders of the macrocosm. A most brilliantly done structure overlooking the city; his heart beating faster as he always desired to find out that even though he has been to Rio more times than he could actually calculate. He looked around tourists, guides; people busy taking photos and making certain that they take the right shot with the only structure in the backdrop.

He took some photographs and came back to the car and said take me to places where I can have a good meal. Along the way to the restaurant, the automobile came in touch with a man running. As shortly as the car hit him, he fell on the ground and Franco got out to giving him helping hand. He assisted him to bear up; he was panting real bad, seemed at all sides and began to play once more. Franco wiped his hand as it had found blood stains as he helped him up.

Franco looked back and bent his attention to the crowd and forgot entirely about what just occurred. The driver was shouting "ver onde você está Indo.. idiota" [Watch where you are going.. idiot] and as he getting back in the car; he suddenly he hears a gun shot. Everybody is moving around to check what happened, the man who was hit and was running away got shot at point blank.

Shocked and Surprised, Franco told himself "not to panic, keep your calm", got back in the car and ask the driver to accelerate away, as he didn't desire his name all the over the tidings. People moving in all directions scared and crying; the driver slowly moved his car and accelerated as he found the space to make a motion and rushed off. He said change of plans, and lead me back to the hotel.

He couldn't think what he just witnessed and couldn't consider that there are in reality people who pour down in cold blood and he believed that was just in the movies; never thought something like this would take place right in front of his optics. It required some time before he could come out of that jar.

He switched on the TV to check the news. Nix close to the hit man shot on any of the news channels. Not in the afternoon news and not in the evening news as well. He was completely baffled, how can this go on; a gunshot that happened right in front of him, in full daylight and nothing about it in any of the news and not even in the newspaper that gets published for the eve. That was quite something else.

He called up the concierge desk and asked for a different car and driver. After some time he came down and fetched in the new car and said take me to Christ Redeemer and on the path, he asked the driver to stop the car as he experienced the precise location of the gunshot. He was surprised to find out that everything was backwards to normal. No evidence of something like this has happened. No blood and people are talking about it.

For a moment there, he thought he was hallucinating and was imagining things as he was under the sun for too long. With a smile he went back to his car and told the driver – Take me to a serious restaurant where I can get the authentic Brazilian food.

A driver with a smile said Sir – You are going to enjoy this place and he brought him to the Marius Restaurant. He enjoyed a repast fit for a king with an aspect to kill – right in front facing the beach.

Subsequently at the hotel, he freshened up and was sorting the clothes for the wash; he discovered something that was falling out of his left jacket pocket.

He got curious and took that out, he understood what he witnessed in the afternoon was real and he was not imagining things. Probably even those ruffians were looking for him.

It was a brown envelope folded and is inserted into the air hole; the envelope has blood stains.

4

Franco was surprised to see that envelope and was not sure what to do with it. He was very uncertain what all of these would go to.

For him, trouble is the last thing that he wanted to get into; not because he was not interested. He was the sort of individual who wishes to invite trouble back in those days; but today he is grown old and weary and he is not interested to go into one. But curiosity will always kill the cat; he desired to recognize what the secret the envelope held, as a man was ready to yield up his life for this.

The brain of a mortal who made money through selling artifacts and went places searching for them couldn't stand the enticement. He was then tempted to open the envelope and discover what it contained.

With great anxiety, he contained the envelope in his hand; started to unfold the folded enveloped, unfolding one side at a time. At one time the envelope was completely open, he was becoming eager to recognize what's inside and the same time the very view of trouble he wanted to put down the envelope and its contents.

Overcoming all thoughts; he ultimately drew up his judgment to get a peek and destroy the contents. One look is not going to do any harm. He finally, put his two fingers to take the contents out and what he saw completely astonished him. Something he was not able to get a head or butt about.

What is it, he thought to himself, is it some sort of a code? A hidden message? Or is it something that he was doing illegally and doesn't want it, to end up in the wrong hands.

He looked carefully again and again, turning the pages upside down and going through the same from all angles. Now trouble was the last thing he had in his mind and first thing was to crack this code.

He has put on his thinking cap. Was not able to understand what it really meant, until he was in the shower thinking about it. Oh! My God, it's a treasure map. But his mind resisted that thought that very minute. It cannot be as the writings are brand new. Well, it has always proved worthy to go behind the trail when I was young, so what's the harm in trying now?

There were random thoughts going on inside his head and just when he thought he had seen it all, this comes his way. He didn't know whether to stand there or run back home.

He came out of the shower, called the room service and ordered for a J&B Rare. His favorite scotch, especially when he has a mind to clear.

Within minutes he could hear the doorbell, the room service guy kept the bottle and the glass on the table. Opened the bill, took his signature with a smile and left the room, with a nod of his head signaling Thank You.

He poured himself a large, took a sip and was at the window starring to the open space and down was the busy roads of Rio de Janeiro. He was thinking about different things and was trying to take his mind of the envelope and its contents.

He was not able to, all the thoughts he thought about was bringing him back to the very same thing; that he needs to decipher the code and run behind it. But in order to do that, he cannot trust no one and he needs to put on his trekking shoes that he had kept away for a very long time and hit the dangerous roads once again.

Before all that, the primary thing would be to get out of Rio and be in a place of serenity to be able to decipher this. And the only place he knew was his home.

He called up the concierge desk; I want a ticket in business class on the next available flight to JFK. Before the other person on the other side could say anything, he disconnected the call.

He was not able to sleep that night, he kept tossing and turning in bed and no sooner he could see some light coming in through his drapes, he got up and started to pack the things that were lying all over the room.

Later, after breakfast, he went straight to the concierge desk, these are the tickets, and that I thought I would use in this journey; I want to cancel everything and ask them to credit the money back into the same account where I booked these from. And now you tell me the status of my ticket to JFK that I called for last night.

You look stressed, the man at the travel desk tried to strike a conversation with him. Franco was not interested. He cut it out right there. Yes! Everything is alright. Something important came up and I need to leave immediately. Also make sure that I have all the arrangements to take the next flight home.

He said next flight to JFK would be leaving in 5 hours, you can go ahead close the formalities here and by the time you get down, you will have your ticket ready and a chauffeur would be here to take you to the airport. Franco smiled and left for his room, on the way he stopped at the reception desk and said please keep my bill ready, I'm leaving in 1 hour.

Some days are just not the same. I can't wait to get home and try to break this thing into a language that I can understand. This was the thought that Franco had when he was taking the elevator and moving into his room to pack his things.

5

As shortly as he drew back to JFK, he hurried out and as he delivered to pre-pond his journey and in his excitement he didn't inform anyone. So he straight went to rent a car with a driver. He stated, he needs a car to Utica, NY.

A long driveway, the limousine services has never got such an offer before and they were happy and obliged. He couldn't wait to get home. A good 4 and half hours drive, he finally reached his destination. As it was a pre-paid service, he just tipped the driver with two $50 bills and got inside his vacation villa before the driver could extend his gratitude.

He opened the house kept his bags in the living room and went straight to his study.

Opened his drinks cabinet and poured himself a neat Glenmorangie Single Malt and opened the letter once again and wore his thinking cap again.

His work was more like a library, surrounded by books of all varieties. There was a study table right in front of a huge picture of his family facing the door. His board was very groovy with a laptop on one position and one pen stand on the other. A notepad, a phone, a small alarm clock and a daily schedule calendar in front; an executive lazy boy chair, a 101 inch plasma TV, on one side and with an amazing vista overlooking the lake through the windowpane.

This was his study room; he comes to this villa when he wants to step away from his busy schedule and only was welcome in this house.

He kept envelope on the table, scanned it and saved it to his laptop on his desk, opened up an application that he usually used to decode things and started to run that application to understand the possible combinations that it can come up with.

As he was waiting for the application to throw up some results, he heard some noise coming from upstairs. He spread a hidden compartment in his desk and removed a gun out and guided it straight and began to run.

Going up one stair at a time, taking a deep breath every time, moved upwards, piling up all the bravery he had within and on his way up, he made certain that the gun was loaded and the guard was off. He got to the doorway where he picked up the noise from. Carefully and to make sure he takes anyone by surprise, he bent the door knob, took him in the room and he scanned the entire room, none was found in that location.

He was confounded and the thought that he might have reckoned it all as he had all his attention diverted to that little page he found within the envelope.

He came down to fit the application, if it has had any results.

He was disappointed to witness the application was not able to crack any of it. He took the telephone to dial his daughter to let her know that he is back in town.

She was surprised to find out that he is back in town. And she didn't expect something like this to happen, she had a lot of questions for him. He cut her off and ordered her, listen, something bad happened, I will send you an email shortly though our family secure server. Remember, trust no one, when the time is right and if need be somebody would contact you and give you our family secret code – Trust him and you will be safe.

6

Ambra came back to her senses with a shiver of shock as the bell rang. She went and peeped through the hole to make sure that she would be safe, if she opens the threshold. It was the mailman, she opened the door and he handed over a cover and asked her to sign.

It was a letter mailed from Turkey. She opened it anxiously; it says:

"Believe in coincidence, my kid. For fate is too much for one to understand, I stand here looking at the sky, wondering, then why am I surprised. You my child is made of gold and it took time for me to understand, what I searched is too far to reach.

Keeping things simple

Starting with 32119, as you remember, down the bushes, into the cave, round about 2nd tunnel, 40 feet deep, beware of the rocks and you need to see it to believe it"

'I may not be alive or would have absconded and would be in a situation that I cannot contact you, if you are reading this letter, because certain truths are supposed to be hidden, while certain others are supposed to be destroyed, I shouldn't have left you alone to start this journey, but you are going to finish it for me.

Trust no one – as I said a man would contact you, but I don't know how, he will give you our family code and you can trust only him'

As the tears fell from her eyes as she read the part that her dad may not be alive. All of this was completely new, for her. I'm going to finish a journey that he started; a man going to contact me but he doesn't know how. Weird, there are only a few options for him to contact me. Email, Phone, Letter, Face to Face and she was trying to make some sense of the letter that she just received.

The tears started to roll down her cheeks as she embraced that letter; it was from her dad.

Is he alive or dead? A question I guess, I need to figure out from everything that is at my disposal. In order to do that, I would need to start walking his path from the very first point he started -The villa in Utica.

She had a lot of things to get actioned upon and her priority was to meet the detective at 7:00PM outside the stadium and the rest of the things could wait.

Without wasting much time, she took her car as she had to reach Utica to meet the detective and her journey would have to start from there.

With a great deal of affairs going on within her, her confused mind was not capable to think straight. She was not able to make sense of anything until she got into her dad's place.

7

It didn't look like a torture chamber, but it had everything that the torture chamber would have. All weapons that is demanded from the ancient Judas chair to the most modern electric chair. You name it and it was in there.

You lost it? What do you mean by you lost it? – This is the second time that you are losing it because of your inefficiency. Last time in Brazil, you didn't get it from the man you shot. This time in Turkey; you guys don't deserve to be here. You kill people thinking you would get it from them and I clean the mess that you make. This is beyond disgusting. I'm not going to take this shit anymore.

Boss, this time, he just burned the clue completely and I was not able to do anything other than killing him, but I haven't left any trace for the officials to find me.

He didn't listen to those words. He bent his head and asked - do you even desire to hold out after being so inefficient and after you made me bow my head down in embarrassment. And as I stand in front of the mirror looking at myself, I feel ashamed that men like you are on my team and from today, I don't have to live with that idea anymore.

Kill him but make sure that he sees the pain of dying before the last breath on his body leaves. And make certain that this message goes loud and clear to all the multitude who are working for me, as it would become worse if they fail me once more. The moral is 'You let me down and you won't see another dawn'.

With that thought Leonardo Carunio left the room.

Leonardo – The last living member of the Carunio mafia clan, 28 years old and the most wanted person by all the colors of the intelligence across the globe; but a free traveler with different fake identities all the time and is very careful, he doesn't use the same alias twice. As the colors of intelligence try their luck to cast him behind bars for good, he always manages to yield them a berth.

The people who entered his arena are not heard about or seen. The search for Leonardo and his people put a great deal of intelligence forces in shame.in shame. While the local police have always supported him for the money that comes to their account for serving him. The intelligence has tried many possibilities to get to him by monitoring the payout to the local cops but he is always careful – the money that he transfers are from an untraceable account or is paid in cash.

People in and around the places that he carries his illegal activities are scared to take his name. A young boy, tall and well built; if not the member of this clan, the most eligible bachelor in town; Masters in history and a masters in astrophysics; a rare breed of education; a rare breed of education combined with a brain for cruelty.

Passed on his studies half way, as his father passed away and he had to take charge of his family business and the people his dad backed up. This occurred as he was about to finish his further studies in Geography.

Forgiveness being the final word or the word that he has forgotten makes him the best at what he is managing.

His crowd of hooligans knew only one thing; what Leonardo says, that's the final word out there, if he had ordered torture; then torture it is.

They started with boiling his bare foot in hot oil, later when they understood, the skin was half boiled, they forced him to walk and sit on a triangular shaped chair, which is also known as the Judas Chair and before that he was stripped while they seated him on that and his crying due to pain increased as he slipped through the pointed area. His hand was tied back while another person was pulling his nails out. A live rat was inserted in his oral cavity as he yelled in pain, so that every time he screamed, the rat would bite his tongue and from then on, his interference was not heard outside the torture chamber.

Later he is pulled out of that chair and his hand was kept in water that is boiling and a bright light is against his eyes so that he would lose his vision. He is left there for a few minutes and then later tied upside down and salt water is poured all across his body and then later he was thrown into the sea, where he is left to die.

Leonardo and his masses were recognized for their cruelty, burying people alive to leaving them to rats half dead. They were ruthless, unforgiving cruel people who walked upon this land.

8

Ambra was getting ready to catch up with the detective. As any rich spoiled kid, she got into her very own Porsche, two seater and drive to the place where they mutually agreed to meet, while in the back of her head it was banging like a gong the words that her father told her; Trust no one.

Even though she was 10 minutes early to reach the venue, Detective Bryne had been already there waiting for her. He was tilting on his car with a half smoked cigarette.

They both nodded and shook hands.

The news that I want to share is not very pleasing, you will have a do a lot of work and put together 1+1=2. Till then all the information I'm giving you is hardly a reference point and zero else.

She was losing her patience, but she was ready to wait as long as it takes before he could share the info about her missing father.

That's ok, said Ambra, share the information and let me attempt to put this together. And if you don't mind, can I record this conversation. Detective Bryne just opposed to the idea of recording and asked her to switch the recording device off. And subsequently a great deal of sentiment, she simply paid up and shifted off the device and what he didn't notice is that, she already had her mobile telephone in her pocket in the recording mode.

Okay, let me start from the very beginning. Your father went missing in the year 2009 and around that time you filed a complaint with us, which set course of an investigation. The investigation that was carried out most diligently by one of our detectives; I see that he traced your father to Brazil and then later to Turkey, somewhere down the investigation, his boss transferred him to another location, another area and of course a different case all together. I attempted to dwell into the details, so that I could update the inside information to you when we gather.

Unluckily, I was unsuccessful to meet data. And so I tried to contact this detective, so I if I could gather further information, but that was a dead end as well. When I checked his file, I see that the access to that was denied. Only then it provoked my curiosity, I searched the databases after databases, but couldn't bring anything further.

The investigation was left there, the file of your father has not moved since.

Then afterwards, last month, the file was moved to us the homicide team as a new routine practice. It's part of a new program, if the missing person's whereabouts is not found in 3 years, the event requires to go forward assuming that he is dead; and usually a detective is assigned immediately, but in this case, none is assigned so far.

And then to reduce the long story short, your father was last visited in Turkey, so thought the detective, prior to that in Brazil that is all that I can help you with.

Thank you very much. Could you please assist me with the name of the investigator who investigated earlier?

Sad that is confidential info that I can't partake. No problem said Ambra. This is my card, call me on my secure line, if you need any help said the detective with a grin.

They shook hands and departed ways.

And when the detective arrived at his car, he wrenched back and said – Oh! The detective never travelled to verify the details of your father's whereabouts all information that he received was from very reliable sources, but I could see someone has manipulated the actual file and some information has been tampered with. But I gave you all information that I'm 100% certain.

This just raised Ambra's eyebrows. She could watch the detective drive away from that situation and she tried to play what has been recorded on her telephone. Unluckily, the recording is not clean and is not able to make out anything, Ambra bent her head in unbelief.

9

Ambra parked her car in the garage and opened the door and went in. She was confused and she had all the rights to be. Daddy has been dropping for the final few years; the police didn't initiate a proper investigation; with all this in her intellect, she was simply not able to focus properly. Even though she knows where dad was sighted last and now as all the doors are closed, it is time for her to use up things in her hand, move ahead with firm grip and set about putting all the components in concert.

She got a spicy coffee and seated down to reckon, she knew, she would be able to infer the details only if she travels the route that her dad had walked before; but she doesn't possess the capabilities, knowledge or know people in business to help her out here.

She recalled the telephone conversation that they had the day he returned from Rio de Janeiro, cutting his long trip short and saying that something bad has happened and I will send you an email through our dependable network.

The email: she thought, in the secure email, which she never opened, which actually dropped off her mind and she cursed herself for answering that.

The email reads: Daughter, do you believe you can handle a mystery? This is not a laughing matter and the earnestness of the issue is way beyond your vision. Mater's got a sharp deviation when I was in Rio, I witnessed a murder and the victim stuck in an envelope in my sack, which I reckon is a map. The map is scanned is there in my personal computer and when you are ready, you would be able to open it with a codification. You will receive help if needed, the benefactor, would contact you in person when he is ready. You will never know when and what is going to happen to me. With the way things are going, I'm eager to understand where this would lead to. I haven't cracked it yet. I will let you know when I do. Kisses.. Dad.

She couldn't understand anything that was happening. Underlined words, what is the importance. She knew one thing; some days later, her father broke the code and has commenced his journey going after his so called treasure. And that was easy to interpret as she recalled the voice mail.

Franco was disappointed as the application didn't throw any results. Weeks and months passed before he could crack the code. In the dawn of May 2009, he was in his living room and there were a few mad magazines lying around, he wanted some relaxation and some laughs, so he took the magazine and started to turn the pages and he saw something that looked like a puzzle that resembled the treasure map he has. He swiftly turned the pages to find out how to snap it.

He hurried back to his study and carried that piece of paper and attempted to break it.

Bingo! And he was able to read the map. He left a message for Ambra on her voicemail. Code cracked, leaving on a journey. You need to be careful, I will call you every day, make sure that the call goes to the voicemail and you don't answer the call. I will be shouting out our residence number, due to any reason I'm not able to call you for three sequential days, it's time for you to panic and make things in action. Be careful and trust no one.

Why does he keep saying that? What sort of a situation is he in? She got a call regularly and as she let it go to voicemail and as long he called, she never bothered. And unfortunately one day, the doom happened, the call stopped and she panicked.

She knew until and unless she continues her presence of mind nothing can be put together and she had to, without a choice, had to think straight.

She began to pen down the events one by one, events that her dad once described, information that she collected from the detective. Nothing made sense, but she knew, eventually it would, this is just the start.

As nobody was able to give her a direction to start from, she just assumed that the wind took her dad. Merely in order to see where the wind failed, she had to know where the wind came from. All she knew was the wind cannot hide for a long time; it will rise sooner or later for her.

And that was a start; she then remembered what detective told her, that he was last discovered in Turkey. What was he doing in Turkey? What did he find there? What sort of a mess did he land in? A set of queries that needed an answer and she didn't know whether to abide on that point for more clear cut direction or take heed to her gut feeling and start a trip to Brazil or Turkey.

And on the spur of the moment, she diverted her attention to the letter that she received from Turkey. She read it over and over again. Dad liked puzzles, but this is too much, at least when he should have kept everything straight. And subsequently a long suspension of thought, she came to a conclusion that, he wanted her to get something; thus when I understand this puzzle, I would be ready to turn over. The search which my dad left unsaid and when I walk that course in which my dad walked, I'll see him. My most treasured treasure - my dad.

A man is going to contact me and he will use the family code, so that I would understand that he is the man who my father entrusted with; a letter that is no help at all.

Was there any other place where my father travelled to? Dad's computer has the scanned copy of that map. She switched that on; the desktop was the picture of her father and her, which was taken when she won her horse race. Tears began to drift downward. She then found out on the desktop itself a file name titled "Treasure Map". She eagerly double clicked it to open and it prompted for a password, she tried all possible combinations but in vain.

She was in half a mind to go online and book her tickets to Turkey. She was uncertain of where to go and that was the sole thing that drew her back. She stated to herself that until and unless something solid surfaces, I cannot move a muscle.

She just made a few calls to check the details of the flight tickets to Turkey, place of stay etc, but she didn't make any reservations.

When she wanted some smart advice, she would always turn to dad and now she was not able to relate anybody in her head who she could trust and who can give her the advice that she was seeking.

It is unquestionably starting to be difficult time to make out with the state of affairs and she knew nobody can take her dad's place. Friends, siblings, mentors, idols, coaches; they all can be many; but father can be only be one and none can take his place.

10

B randon got his hot cocoa along with him to his study and placed it along the table near him. He read the missive in his workforce with keen rarity; with a silver envelope opener that he possessed, he opened the missive. He was very surprised to learn that the letter came from his friend, a person whom he trusts with his life and the only person who knows about his whereabouts.

The letter reads:

My Dear Friend – You are receiving this letter because, you are the only person I trust and you are the only one who would be able to help and I could think of none other in this dire circumstance. If you are receiving this letter it either means that I'm dead or I'm in trouble. On a recent trip to Brazil, I came across a decoded message, which took me some time to crack it. You know me, I would go behind anything that impresses me or gives me a challenge and this one was neither. This one was different; it not only impressed me, but also challenged me. And I started my journey, without learning about the dangers that this involved.

Right now, I'm unsure the state of my daughter and I want you to give her a helping hand. She would be in trouble as well. I'm sure she would start using her means to find me. And I completely understand the requirement from her perspective. I want you to find her, stop her from doing that and most importantly protect her from everything that might come her way.

Knowing her, she should be in half a mind to start the journey. Don't be late.

When you contact her you would require 32119

Franco Gallo.

Brandon didn't know what needs to be done. He knew one thing, that he needs to protect his daughter from all dangers by hook or by crook and there are no two ways around it.

He interpret the letter once again and didn't know where to look for her. But he had an email sent from Franco few years back, tracking down the IP address would be a starting point, he thought.

Tying it back to the computer and understanding the connection details and further tracking down the address of the location with all the gadgets that he holds in his possession that would be a cake base on balls. Without wasting much time, he started his task.

Within no time, he was able to trace the location of the computer and to his surprise the computer was active at that point of time.

Ambra, on the other side without knowing the dangers that await her; she was searching for the flight timings, locations and was trying to build herself a map and an itinerary for her journey to find her father. She was fixed and she had cleared up her judgment that she is working to arrange a journey on the trail that her father walked, and set forth an investigation that the cops didn't pursue or showed interest in. After all, it's her father who is missing.

As she was tasting all the possible permutation and combination to break the code that her father has locked using a password for the map, she was unable to unlock it with a million tries.

All of a sudden, a window popped on to her computer for a chat – It reads, don't do anything stupid. She didn't reply to that request, she just shut down that window.

The window appeared again – it read – 32119 – Does that mean anything to you?

She knew instantly that, this is the person whom her father was talking about.

She replied: Yes! It does and I know I'm talking to a person who my dad said would contact me when the time is right.

Brandon: Yes! I'm doing to you, should reach in less than 24 hours, do not act or fix any determinations in a headlong fashion, let me come and we will spill the beans.

Ambra: Ok. I'll wait here.

The screen reads, connection terminated by the host.

Now Brandon knew exactly where she is and what she has been doing. Even though, he disconnected the chat session, he was still browsing through Franco's computer without her knowledge that he was doing something like that. He required to be certain that nobody else is counting into that computer. He copied a lot of files from that one of his along with the file named: "Treasure Map" that he thought might come in handy later.

He disconnected the connection and then he booked the air tickets that would take him to Ambra at the shortest possible time.

11

What Ambra didn't know was that he was actually coming to stop her from doing what she was going to do. As per the instructions he received, Brandon is supposed to stop her from risking everything and going out in the open looking for her father.

She was anxious and confused at the same time, as she doesn't even know the name of the person who is coming to assist her, forget about the rest of the details but at least the name? She had her own thoughts and how she is going to recognize him when he rings the bell?

On the flight, Brandon was trying to check all the documents that he copied from Franco Gallo's computer. Everything had dates, plans, what he intended to do and of course certain documents were of no help as it pertained to his business. All but one he was able to open, apart from the file named "Treasure Map". Additionally it is password protected.

He tried all possible combinations to get it open, as he knew Franco very well; he started with his date of birth, other details and everything but was in vain.

He had a few hours to kill before he reached his destination. He closed his laptop and tried to rest. His mind was at work, trying to recollect the contents of the letter.

These words from the letter kept haunting him; *"If you are receiving this letter it either means that I'm dead or I'm in trouble. On a recent trip to Brazil, I came across a decoded message, which took me some time to crack it."*

He spread out his eyes, got hold of the laptop and opened that file again, it prompted for the password. He thought to himself, would it be so easy; let me give it a try. He typed in B-R-A-Z-I-L and bingo the file opened. If seeing is believing; he just saw a map that gave Franco the challenge to venture out risking his own life. But again, he used his applications that he had assumed that it would crack the code. Unsuccessful with that, he shut the laptop again and attempted to think of other possible ways to break the code. Paleontology being his major and his interest, it afforded him an idea rather to help Ambra rather than restraining her in a close hold.

He started thinking of many different reasons why not to go behind the map; but nothing was able to convince his heart, which was pounding for adventure which he was longing to get.

Leonardo, in his mansion was sitting inside his bedroom facing the sea; thinking about other ways to get the copy of the that piece of paper that Franco burned in Turkey. Leonardo only knows that such a thing exists, but he has no idea what the content of that is. He was cogitating about the content and where it would lead, the last thing he knows that the person who sustained that was last discovered in Turkey. Then that should be my starting spot, but from there where to? The question kept his cruel mind busy like a fireball that was burning in the water. But he had a starting point, he doesn't even know what that piece of paper contained, what brought Franco to Turkey with that piece of paper? And why didn't he part with it? What was so important in that paper, that he protected that with his life? He was confused, but with all that was happening, he very well knew that somebody someday will come looking for that person who got killed and he assumed that he would be able to get the details that he is looking for from that person or so he wished.

He came to be known about this from his father on his dying bed, including his father and others who drew it down has no estimate what it leads to or what it is. None of them were able to crack the code. When he got his hands on this piece of thing, he wanted to be the first one who actually tried to find the inner meaning of that. Without having a second look at the content, he handed it over to his most trusted friend, who in turn tried to escape with it as he knew he could make money selling that piece of paper as it was passed down generations and it had that antique value. Which even today, he regrets.

While attempting to flee with that, his other guards tracked him down and tore him down in Brazil.

12

The door bell gave a fright to Ambra; she slowly moved towards the door and moved the drapes to check who is outside. Someone who is in his early fifties, well built and well dressed. Not a familiar face, though. He caught her looking through the windowpane, he smiled and waved for which she didn't reciprocate. And she had the entire right not to. She was frightened away as scared can be.

He rang the bell again, nervous as she can be, she slowly opened half the door and if need be she can be quick in closing it as well. Brandon smiled and said I'm Brandon; I'm the one who communicated with you over the computer and told you that I was coming.

She was saved; she spread the door and welcomed him in. Brandon slowly pulled out the letter that he received and handed it over to Ambra so that she can go through that just to make sure she trusts him completely.

They had to have trust with each other which would make it easy on his way forward.

She went through the letter and, as she folded the letter she said you know what, I cannot be in a protective custody, there is no way that you are going to stop me. I have to go and find my dad; I'm all he has and I will make sure that I find him. I desire to know what took place and there are no two ways around it.

Wow! That really broke the ice, Brandon thought.

If that's how you want to play it, I'm game; with my experience and knowledge, combined with your brains, I'm sure we can crack this. But what we need is a starting point. Without that, I'm not letting you leave the house.

We do have a starting point. She narrated the conversation that she had with the police, made him take heed to all the voicemails. So investigation stopped in Turkey, That's a starting level, but in order for us to proceed farther, our chief goal should be to go after the police who did the initial investigation and we need to obtain further inside information. Until and unless, we cannot start a trip, because all we deliver is a hunch that he would be in Turkey and hunch is a little more concrete, because this letter that I received was posted from Turkey. All assumptions apart, let's run down the police officer who did the investigation. Meet him and then we will go.

But how are we going to manage that? I don't yet have a name. No worries; Let me worry about that, while you find us a transport to move around everywhere you go. And make sure that you are not using your credit card for any transaction. We need money, liquid money for the journey and make sure you are not going to use your credit card to buy anything from now on, not even an airline ticket. In case if anybody is playing along, usually in these circumstances there are going to be other people involved. I don't want them to follow us because we made a wrong move.

From my past experience in the military, I would say, we need a plan and we need to be making sure that we are more than careful with every step we take. I want you to arrange a transportation, brand new phone connections, etc. Give me some time and let me try to figure out who this investigating officer was and his whereabouts.

Brandon took out his laptop connected to the internet using the Ambra's cable connection and also connected to different other networks just to make sure that he is not tracked, even if someone is tracking him, he wanted to buy some time before anyone could track him down.

Once he made sure that his connection is secure, he got connected to the Police Department Database,

Enter User name and Password to proceed; he clapped his hands and said now we are in business. With his new toys and other software applications breaking into the Police Department Database was a cake walk.

Once the access was granted, he set about using Key Words to locate the file of Franco Gallo, he typed the name, Brazil, Turkey – a batch of info but nothing helped him to locate the file of Franco Gallo. After hours of search he was not able to get any information.

Then he thought, it would be better to search with Ambra's name as she is the one who filed the complaint. He typed in Ambra Gallo – And that search popped the results and it also opened multiple files. He kept all those filled into his local system so that he can work through them in detail subsequently. He also used his time on the network to get other updates like Franco Gallo, known associates, usual contacts, who all were questioned and who all were held at the station under protective custody or for further interrogation. Once he received all the information that he was looking for, he disconnected his main connection, while keeping the other zombie connections on for some more time until he unplugged his computer. And as he disconnected the computer, he wrote down the name of the detective who initially looked into this case and his last known address.

13

Unable to locate where the search was happening from in the Police database as there were hundreds of zombie connections; Leonardo was losing his hope of finding the map or the whereabouts of the person who was killed by one of his hooligans.

He got his gun and started shooting aimlessly into the open just to grow away from his frustration. He called one of his men later that day and said I want to know about that person who was killed in Turkey, where is he from, why did he go to Turkey and the only person who knew all this is now in a pool of blood in my basement as he was following him from the time he reached Turkey, I should have thought about this before killing him and should have tried to extract as much as information from him rather than just taking a decision to finish him off.

Was he working alone? Did anyone else accompany him? He asked. None, he was operating solely on this one as we wanted to keep this a secret and not many people are aware what he managed to obtain this sought of punishment. All they know is that he did something really terrible.

Could you ask someone to check the address that of that guy, he might have given it in the hotel when he took his room, most probably it would be fake, but we would have a starting point? And also, we have his address in Utica, we had him under surveillance there. I require this info as soon as possible, let us try to keep this confidential until we receive more than adequate proof.

Every bit I was trying to search, the police database, I could witness someone else was looking for any other information in the database which was linked to an external network. I was not able to zero in on that target. I think the search tab said Ambra Gallo. Try getting some information about her as well. In all likelihood, that might contribute to a new door, which can throw some light to us. We need to find a way to get that map or someone who has already deciphered that.

Boss why do you keep calling that a map? I have a feeling that it is a treasure map that he didn't want to lose it in the wrong hands. Hence he destroyed it or was even willing to risk his life for that. This is just a guess and I may be wrong.

The satire of the post was that, Brandon came in for a different charge and had to begin a fresh one. And to crown it all, the knowledge that he has about Paleontology and relics are all bookish, none of them came from years of experience. And this would be his first mission on such a subject. But his niche skill in martial arts and surviving in utmost conditions all of that came from his years of experience, which was good enough for him to start a journey such as this. But the very thought of responsibility that Ambra is travelling along with him made him nervous, as never before, he had an experience of someone else's life in his hands before.

As shortly as he disconnected all the zombie connections, Ambra walked in and said I have a difficult time making sure that all the payments are made through cash as I'm not having sufficient amount with me. The only way that I can think of is using the ATM and withdraws as much as cash as possible and dump the card.

Brandon didn't approve that idea of using the ATM. He said check, do you have any checks here. I do on my dad's account and mine. Get the checkbooks, Brandon said. Ambra searched her dad's draw and got the checkbook and gave it to Brandon. Brandon opened the customized leather cover with the imprint of Franco's initials FG; a letter fell out. It reads

Brandon – I knew that my daughter would lead you into this and I could sense your idea and I would have done the same thing for a daughter in a desperate state. Hence, I have signed a couple of checks, use that and withdraw the money, don't use her account as it might be tracked. Mine they won't in case I'm captured or in trouble, my account would be the least of their worries.

He read the letter, with a grin passed it over to Ambra. Now, before we head out. I want you to pack all the things that would be required for this journey, including a compass, a diary a pen and a pencil. And for the rest of the stationary I will make the necessary arrangements. We need to keep everything ready here and then we will head to the Bank the first thing tomorrow as it's already late and none of the banks would be open at this point of time.

Ambra nodded her head in agreement.

So what's for dinner? Brandon inquired.

I was not expecting someone to knock on the door and ask for food, might have some eggs and some juice in the refrigerator.

Keep your bags ready, we will start as soon as the bank opens.

Where to inquired Ambra – Well let's say, our first destination is the bank and then we head to the detective who was taking charge of the investigation earlier and then we will determine where our next block would be, probably Brazil, where your dad found the map. As it say's Brazil, we will start from there. We will buy our tickets at the airport. And remember, we are tourist and would be using different names throughout the journey. In case, we cross paths with anyone we know – You are my new girlfriend and in case none of them cares, we are just tourists who met on the plane who had some good time together.

Ambra had been already nervous as she could be and this just added to the pressure. She wanted to ask why all this and why we can't reveal our identities? A question that she knew the answer to, partially; Brandon wanted to keep it that way and provide her with just enough information. And he wanted to keep it that way because, it's always a better idea if she doesn't have all the information as Brandon knew to an extent what all are the hurdles that he is going to come across in this journey.

14

Leonardo was not able to sleep that night, with a lot of memories of his father and moreover, he lost something that his father handed over to him for safe keeping that was there with the Carunio family through generations. Totally unaware of the contents, Leonardo was more inclined towards the antique value of the piece rather than anything.

He could see the sun through his window, rising among the other stars that he was not able to see; that wondrous sight that he missed for a long time now. He was awake throughout the night, but he was not tired. Around 8:30AM, he heard a knock on his door and the door opened, it was his butler with his morning coffee, he was not supposed to be disturbed before that and that was the order that was followed without any exception. The only exception is when there is any kind of emergency. So far, none has come.

The surprising sight for the butler was that, Leonardo hadn't changed his clothes from last evening and he was wide awake. Without uttering any word, Leonardo signaled the butler to mix his coffee to which he obliged. After handing over the coffee, the butler left his room and closed the door behind him.

He took a sip from the cup looking outside; the sun is now shining bright as ever, strong and lively. Without any complaints it stood there in the sky, throwing its rays all over.

Leonardo was in his room not able to make a call on what he needs to do. All he could now think of is about Ambra Gallo, the name he saw while trying to connect to the police database and about the artifact that he came across and lost as he handed it over to the man he trusted the most.

Around noon, he had a knock on his room and he didn't bother to answer, he heard the knock again which he ignored. His mobile started to ring; it was one of his men trying to reach him. He disconnected the call, it was silent for some time, but it started to ring again. It was the same man, he answered, but didn't say anything, and he heard the voice asking him permission to come inside the room. Leonardo said yes and disconnected the call.

The door opened again for the second time that day. Two of his men walked in and they were surprised as well, he hasn't changed his clothes from last evening, haven't brushed or taken a shower. And he had that look on his face that said it better be important.

Leonardo sat on his chair, legs crossed and his hands were on the desk waiting to hear from them. On a usual day, he would have asked "what's it about?" but not today, he was just silent and waiting for them to open up.

With a little stammering one of them slowly started, we got the whereabouts of that lady, Ambra Gallo. On hearing that name, Leonardo slowly rose from his seat. And the other person continued, he is the daughter of that guy, who was killed in Turkey last year, she has lodged a complaint with the police that her father went missing 3 years back, now the case is handled by the homicide missing persons and due to our influence, the things have died down and the case has not proceeded further.

But she is not a computer wizard to check through the database through a different computer outside, as all rich spoilt kids, she has been raised with a lot of pampering and by that guy alone. Mother died during her first year and she has been good with her academics.

Leonardo didn't say anything. He went silent for a long time. After some time, he said let's track her. If she is not a computer wizard, then she has a helper, let's keep our eyes open and slowly and steadily, let's keep her under over surveillance. Please make all the arrangements for that, from this very moment, I want to know who she meets, where she is going, what she is doing, anything and everything should pass through me. And when it's time, I will let you know and that's the time, we are going to bring her in, till that time let them think, they are scot-free.

15

You haven't taken down anything and how are you going to remember things, Ambra asked Brandon. I think that's a talent that I deliver, whatever I experience even through the niche of my eye, I recall. Names, faces, numbers, symbols, etc., you name it, I can remember and I can recall that when I wanted to, but at certain occasion, it just might take the time that's all. Old age is slowly sneaking in I guess. That is the reason why I jot down the important ones, especially this name and address of the person whom we are going to meet today's post going to the bank.

We will cash in these checks and you also carry some of yours just in case, they ask. And post meeting that detective we have another stop to make, meeting an old friend of mine and that is also equally important.

The bank was crowded than usual, Brandon only hoped that they are not followed from the very first step, but we cannot be sure. As they wanted to withdraw large amounts, so Ambra and Brandon took two separate lines and reached the cashier's desk at different points and they withdrew money at different intervals just to avoid any tension. As soon as they withdrew money, Brandon took an envelope and inserted 5000 dollars into that and sealed it. This is for my friend when we meet him. Ambra raised her eyebrows in confusion and distrust at the same time. She didn't say anything at that point, but wanted to wait till they get there.

The door bell rang and a man dressed in proper suit, old but classy opened the door. How can I help you? Asked him, we are here to meet Detective O'Connell. Oh! But he is not here, you might find him at the Swank Club, if you are lucky or you can try his yacht, the name of his yacht is Observe and you are? Inquired Ambra, I'm the butler, miss. Ambra nodded.

And in a distance, Brandon saw the photograph of this detective and he understood, the person that he is looking for the and his dear friend is the same person, he handed over the sealed cover to Ambra and said it looks like this is not required, the detective that we are looking for and the person I want to meet later is the same person and he is rich, bribing won't work. Ambra grinned.

They proceeded to the Swank Club, Ambra was just following Brandon on the way, and she asked what Swank is? Brandon said we are just about to find out.

As they arrived at the club, she understood what Swank is – it would be another name for Classy. This was the club for the elite. How could that detective who might have made a maximum of 90,000 dollars a year could yield something like this? Ambra wondered but not Brandon, he thought to himself, she is not a good listener, I just told her that he is rich.

They both directed towards the reception and rang the bell – a lady clothed in red appeared, how may I serve you sir? Brandon was mesmerized for a couple of minutes until Ambra gave a nip and she started, hi we would love to meet Mr. O'Connell and we assume he is one of your members. Oh! Which one would that be Kevin O'Connell or Ryan O'Connell, that would be Kevin said Brandon. He is unquestionably one of our members and usually he is here during this time, but alas, he hasn't been here this week. Can I take a message or let him know his friend's name that came to... before she could finish, Brandon inquired, where can I find him? Do you have any idea?

She just smiled and said I'm sorry, I wouldn't have a clue. Brandon smiled and said that's ok, probably we will be in luck the next time we come in. He grabbed Ambra's hand and walked out. Next stop his yacht. Ambra was already becoming impatient and he could see that. He said Patience my dear.. Patience that is what is required more than anything in this journey; we would have to squander a lot of money and a lot of time because nothing is easy and free in this world. So let's pray that at least he is there at his yacht.

Detective Kevin O'Connell, who took his early retirement was lazing in his yacht trying to spend his morning time with newspaper and regular coffee. He was a decent cop hailing from a moneyed household. "To Serve and to Protect", he wanted to be the best. When the department required him to bend things and which arrived from the very top, he gave over his badge and gun in pride and walked off. Not a lot can afford to execute that, but because he possessed the wealth of only kings had, he didn't pause. And moreover, that was not the meaning he held for the phrase "To Serve and to Protect"

He took his morning paper in his hand and took the coffee that he brewed out of the coffee machine. He took his first sip and then put on his sunglasses and opened the paper and was about to start reading,

Detective Kevin O'Connell, he heard someone asking for his name, he got up and peeped from his yacht, he saw a beautiful young lady accompanied by a bit elderly well built guy. Even though, his heart skipped a beat, he waited patiently for them to arrive and visitors were the last thing he expected on such a beautiful morning.

16

There were monitors and speakers and different kinds of state-of-the-art gadgets that filled the room. You name it you had in that room and 3 tech experts trying to decode different things. This was the room where the Leonardo surveillance team sits.

They were all illegal, they had access to all the colors of intelligence, access to their database, they can switch on and off any camera across the globe, type in keywords, all of the transactions and whereabouts regarding that keyword would pop up, face recognition software, blood analyzer to DNA profiles, sound Isolators to video feed recorders he had all the types of gadgets that he would require. The list of the most wanted people across locations and their last known address. All information that he requires is there at his fingertip. But of course, things like these all have disadvantages, he would be able to view things only if there is a camera installed, if he has to use a satellite and zoom in on the details, where there are no camera's there would be a snag, things that wants to see the most often happens where there are no cameras and he has to rely on a live vocal feed through a phone.

He didn't hold a DNA or the fingerprint of Franco, else it would have been comfortable for him to peg down the search and get the most of all that he wants.

He took in his surveillance team to supervise every moment of Ambra and her ally. They were attempting to find the identity of the man who she is with and trying to find his whereabouts using the facial recognition software. And the search for him is on in the entire database they had access to. They didn't get any hit from the most wanted or dangerous people. They didn't bother to look through the employee database. If they had, they would have got the details of the Brandon within no time. Sometimes brain ceases to exist while computers over power them. Making them think, that's the last thing. When your search doesn't yield any effect, we try different phrases, but not different places.

Leonardo was growing impatient as they moved along. They were not able to identify where they went from the bank, this time, he didn't want to take any chances, so he thought the best way to make them feel secure is if he didn't send anybody following them and he knew that every now and then they would pop in the camera and he would know their whereabouts and what they are up to.

Impatience grew; the clock is marking and he doesn't deliver a clue who is the man protecting Ambra, all he knows is that Ambra is the daughter of the man who was shot down by one of his ruffians. He really does not know anything else. And the less he knew the more troublesome he became, he was upset and he was mentally unfit to make any decisions. He wanted to know what she knows and he wanted to know why and who is protecting her and what he knows. He knew that the artifact was burned before that guy was killed. And now he is unsure what they want and what is that they are looking for.

Leonardo took his stash of drugs from his pocket, he made a straight line on his right hand, and he brought his hand towards his nose and one long breath and without wasting a pinch everything just went in. We are looking at the wrong place, we are looking at the wrong place; he heard one of his men shouting. He asked what is that they are looking for is.

They misplaced something and they are not able to find it, something that was personal for him. Leonardo was not in a mood for small affairs and definitely was not in a mood to enjoy the little matters. Just ask them to shut up. I didn't get any sleep and I don't think I will until I get some answers, until then just ask them not to irritate me.

But these words, we are looking at the wrong place, kept haunting him. Suddenly, he turned his head to the tech guys and said please use the facial recognition tool to search for the man who is with Ambra in the employee database of all forces in the country and with his age, I should say both active, inactive and as a matter of fact, also look for them in the confirmed dead category.

The key words were fed in and the facial recognition software started scanning all the photos in the employee database of all the types of forces. One by one, the scanning was in progress.

Without blinking, Leonardo was looking at the monitor and after a 2 hour search, it got a hit with the United States Army database and the details were in front of him.

17

He took his hand towards Brandon; I'm O'Connell, Kevin O'Connell. It looks like we know each other, I know you from some place, have we worked together before? For a moment, Brandon and Ambra stood there in silence. Brandon looked at Ambra and then towards Kevin, you have forgotten, we have been on a mission once long back before you left the Army and joined the Police force, as you always wanted to be closer to home. At least now I guess you are happy and you had nothing to lose, apart from a very promising life in the Army.

Brandon Brookes and Kevin, took him close gave a hug and forgot all about Ambra, both of them went back in time to their days and started talking about incidents that they shared together, laughs and gossips that they shared when they were in the force together. They talked about guns, escapes and lots of things about war and training and a lot about their common interests.

Ambra, in the meantime was looking round the yacht, astonished to discover all the gears that he possessed. And hours passed and it didn't look like they were going to discuss about the main reason why they came to meet Kevin and Kevin on the other hand was so indulged and happy that he had a visitor after a very long time. And you could understand that because every now and then, he was offering both Brandon and Ambra things to drink and a lot of eatables.

All of a sudden, Ambra jumped into their conversation and said Sorry that I jump in, but the actual reason that we came to see you is….

Ya! Brandon, why do you come to meet me after all these years and there has to be a reason. And tell me why you were hiding from the rest of the world for such a long time.

Been hiding for a reason which at this point of time I don't want to disclose and why I'm here to meet you is something that we will discuss now.

While you were serving in the PD, there was a missing case of Franco Gallo, the smile on that was there on the face of Kevin slowly faded. She is Ambra, the daughter of Franco and we are here to understand what you know about that missing and why was it untouched even though it was moved to the homicide team.

Kevin slowly took his glass from the table, went straight to the bar counter, and poured him a drink from his very own collection. He took a sip and turned towards them who were eagerly waiting to hear something from him that would actually help them in the rest of their journey.

He averred, I was simply not capable himself and I was moved to another investigation before I could finish or even polish off my first cycle of investigation and that was the last event that I ever had to look into. Post that, I wished, that I never left the Army because I came to know about a world that existed for a long time and will continue to exist as long as the clock is ticking. And for generations to come, they will too go on the path, the path of depravity.

Let's leave it at that said Kevin.

No, I can't leave it there, because we are letting the cat out of the bag about my father here and I would wish to know what has happened to him and in case, if anything has happened I want to recognize the cause why. And I wouldn't rest until I get an answer, if not from you, I will travel the same path that my father did and I'm sure along the way, I would understand the reason why my father disappeared.

Kevin came close to Ambra, as close as Ambra could smell the breath of whiskey that is faring out of his lip. You really want to know why? Well your father might be dead by now and that's the reason why he is not coming back.

She couldn't believe her own ears. She shook her head in disbelief. Her eyes were red and watery. What? She shouted and this time it was loud enough for the people in other yachts to peep over and perk their curiosity to lend an ear to understand the conversation that is happening in Kevin's yacht.

Believe you me; he might be dead by now. That's the intensity of the situation at hand. When you opened that complaint in our department about your missing father, we tried to contact him in more ways than one. And none of those things worked for us to get in touch with Franco. Then we began checking all domestic and international flight passenger lists to determine whether he was in any of that. And his name came up in a flight to Brazil and then we began running for his passport trail. He used his passport in Brazil, Turkey, back in Brazil and from there the trail ended. So my team and I went to Brazil to check the whereabouts, he checked in one of the most expensive hotels there and then moved to Turkey the following day and 1 week later, he was back in Brazil and that time, he didn't lease a room in any of the expensive, inexpensive hotels or not even in a room that a person with $10 could afford. He vanished into thin air. But when tried to verify with the immigration team about his entry back into Brazil, we were surprised, someone else used his passport to get into the country and the officers didn't raise a red flag. We were certain that he is a black cat in the department. But we were out of our jurisdiction.

Only when we were in Brazil, we asked the Hotel people for the messages that he might have had. They all pronounced, he obtained just one message and the message stated, throw it back to me or else you will fail. And I guess the reason why you are here in front of me still looking for your father is that he has not returned and which gives me the suspicion that he is no more and it also tells me that he has not returned what he was supposed to return and I have no clue what he was hiding and what they required.

We attempted to find out where the message came from, but it was from a public telephone and we were not able to narrow down the hunt. It was a mystery.

Then, when I put in a request to head to Turkey from Brazil, we were told that we do not even have the right to be on this case and we are just travelling and more important, Brazil or Turkey, we do not have any jurisdiction in those places. But it was a hunch and I took my permission for my travel only when I boarded the aircraft and I told my chief that we are just sightseeing and even that trip was not taken care by the department. It was just my inquisitive nature that took us there. But we had to give a written explanation about this case and why we were in Brazil. And I have been enjoined to remove my work force out from the situation that it might burn and simply like a reflex action. Only I was not convinced about the lawsuit or the reason what my officials gave me to get me off this shell. As I was still on the case, while I travelled to Brazil as part of the case and as I didn't inform the right officials and took permission, I was asked to go on leave indefinitely without pay as part of the punishment.

I took my badge and I took my gun and kept it on the table and I said I quit and I walked out. I was not convinced, but I was happy, that my trip shook some people who were concerned that this case shouldn't be followed and like cowards they took me off this shell.

Even today, I think about it and all I can give you is the stead where he detained at that period of time or the initial visit post which I cannot tell you anything. You have Brandon with you. You would be safe and I know whatever happens, nothing will befall you until Brandon's last breath is expired. I have that much faith in him.

Ambra couldn't speak for some time. All she could give Kevin was a look through her weak eyes. Befuddled as to what needs to be executed next. And what she is going to do, in case if her father is really dead.

18

She was losing her balance, as if all the veins that run her line were running dry. She couldn't feel herself, she was turning pale. She sat down in one corner of the yacht weeping and as the waves hit the shore and with the silence of the winds, nobody could hear her crying.

Kevin continued as she was crying, as I said he might be dead by now and right now I do not have enough evidence or facts to tell you this in confidence, but you should consider the inevitable.

SHUT UP..... SHUT UP KEVIN, Ambra shouted.

That's Mr. O'Connell to you my dear and the only living person who I thought have vanished from this face of earth is Brandon and nobody else.

DO I LOOK LIKE I CARE.. Please SHUT UP.

Kevin got irritated and moved to his cabin pouring himself another drink.

Brandon, slowly approached Ambra, sat on his knees, kept his hand on her shoulder. I knew this would happen or this is something that you would hear as we embarked on our journey. He said might be, which means we still have something to hope for, but as we move from here, you should keep that in mind, that the inevitable might have already taken place. And whatever the case is, we will try to find your father. If not him, at least we would know why and who. The two questions that we necessitate to find an answer to and without which our journey is incomplete.

I'm not sure whether I want to continue this journey, I can live in the hope that he might return one day. But again, on the contrary Ambra, we must continue the search. He wanted you to come and search for him even though he wanted you to be secure in that house and if he really wanted that, he wouldn't have sent you all those cues. He wouldn't have sent for me to protect you, because only when deadly things combine, we deliver a solution. I arrive with a full scope of experience and you come from a father who has taught you many things and to handle things the way it needs to be treated. He has taught you many things consciously and you have experienced a lot of affairs and have read a great deal of things unconsciously. And I know this how? The minute I entered your house, you welcomed me with a gun; that is fully loaded and was in a position to paint the wall with my brain. Even though you were hiding it behind you. You know that how? He taught you that and there is nothing on this earth that can replace the love a father towards a daughter and he has prepared you well in-order to continue his legacy. What he started and he always wanted you by his side not just as a daughter but as his successor. Nobody might have enjoyed such affection from a father. Keeping in mind the inevitable that you would come to know with a fact, one day, I believe we should go on. Only in case you still desire to quit this journey I'm with you. We will go back home as nothing has happened, thinking that you will be safe inside that four walls. But how far will you dwell your life feeling scared and haunted and with the notion that somebody is watching you?

The decision is yours and only yours, I'm here to ensure that your decision is protected, whatever it may be.

Ambra wiped her cheeks, got up and ran straight to Kevin's cabin. Without uttering a word, without asking for permission, she took a glass poured herself a JB Rare, one shot, poured another one and took another shot, poured herself the third and before she could finish that shot, Kevin stopped her. I can see what you are living through, but adopting a decision with the assistance of alcohol is not dying to resolve the issue. You need to think in peace and you need to think twice and then think again, analyze it and then take your call. No hasty decision. We have taken a number of decisions in our lifetime. Crazy ones, stupid ones, hasty ones, but a lot of us, including Brandon had to pay for the decisions that we made. Why do you think he went into hiding for such a long time, without showing his face to the rest of the world and keeping his very existence a secret? Why, all because of the decisions that he made. But again we didn't sustain a choice, when facing an enemy on a battlefield, we had to get to decisions inside the time frame of snap sound reached our ears and we don't have the liberty of thinking about the after effects or reactions of our conclusions.

Ambra, you have the greatest strength of all by your side, Brandon. That is going to be your advantage and your greatest weapon. Use it wisely.

I advise that you get into a room, think about the after effects of both the possibilities. What will take place if you don't go on this journey and what will bump if you chose to go on this journey? All the pros and cons put it down and analyze what you want to do.

And if Brandon is on the job, I wouldn't hesitate in joining this team because this is one case that has always haunted me and of all the cases I have handled, the one that comes with the pressure and riddles all across the case. I would be honored to unite a squad without any conventions and without anybody whom I need to report to.

And with Brandon, I cognize that he had to go down before someone can even look at us. And you have two us before anybody can look at you. Then get to that room, relax and opine about it. I want you.. No.. We want you to think about this over and over and over again until you are going to open that door against us to let us hear your decision. This is your call sweetie, go ahead and make that call.

Ambra took that final shot of JB and went to that room, closed the door and locked it.

She sat on that large cozy bed of Kevin's and thought for a while. Slowly stood up, moved to the washroom and washed her face and placed upright in front of the mirror. And said Dad, I'm coming for you and I'm not going to let you down.

I'm Ambra Franco Gallo.

19

The monitor showed the results of Brandon Brookes and before Leonardo was able to read or save the scripts, the monitor read, unauthorized access of database, self destruction commences in 5 seconds. And before he knew it, the monitor said files have been erased and no results found.

Leonardo was not even able to read the name of the person who was helping her. And the answers he received were in the Army database through the facial recognition software.

Leonardo's anger knew no bounds, he threw away his phone and it landed on the ground in pieces. Well, at least now that is the last of his phone and the records about Brandon Brookes.

He abruptly turned around and said I've heard about cache, please tick if any of the files that were displayed been automatically kept in cache. There's got to throw some clues that we could get in order to amaze along with our acquaintances along their journey. I'm positive that she is running in circles to find about her father and she doesn't know the danger that awaits them.

Sir, if the files were destroyed it means, they possess a backup server with all the inside information, and it's precisely that we have accessed some confidential information. I attempted to beat us back online to their servers, but I'm unable to relate to their ghost network to regain all the relevant information that is needed.

I do not take no for an answer, find me something and from there like Jack, who found his bean stalk, I will climb until we figure out what and how we can tackle him.

One thing is for sure, if he is in the Army database, he is trained for combat and such a person would be difficult to defeat but not impossible, just difficult. Wish I could lay my hands on his file to see his contacts and known associates, but now that is not possible, we need to find out a way to get his details. And another important matter, if the files were self erased when we looked into the assorted data, which implies he is very important and is classified, he would be a potential threat if he is helping her stay on the journey. We cannot underestimate him at any level. He would be thoroughbred in the Army, this is hardly a wild guess, because this is the first time, the files were auto deleted when we accessed their database. We have done this a zillion times and this is the first time.

Just check, if we are still able to connect to that server which we connected earlier.

Yes! Sir, we are capable to connect to that server, but unfortunately, that files have been scored out and we are not able to find in any of their servers right now, which means, they possess a ghost server in which these classified information are maintained.

The only thing, which we were able to recover from our cache, is his name. He is Brandon Brookes. I just googled him and the results are scary.

He has led as a commanding officer in many of the combats and has successfully completed all the missions that were assigned to him and in places that are again classified. Now this thing is scary, the last known details about him. He has been badly wounded in one of the combats and was dreaded that he would lose his spirit. Later, he vanished into thin air after leaving the force 10 years back. The armed forces have confirmed him dead as there was no news about him for over 7 years.

He has been trained by the Army and by the marines. A lethal combination, his interests are weapons and Paleontology. We were not able to narrow down the hunt any further and were not able to find any further info. This is our only information about him and that too got it from several hits over the internet.

But one thing is for sure, just as you mentioned, it is going to be slightly difficult for all of us to defeat him, but not impossible. We cannot underestimate his talent, which implies we all needs to be extra vigilant.

At this point of time, we know about him, but not the other way around, which gives us an edge above him. We need to allow him play so that we would know what he knows. Keep showing him the cheese and let's chase the black eyes.

We need to prevent the ball rolling and he will sooner or later get the bait and we will see what need to do in order to make him spill the beans. Until then, let him be free, but keep an eye on where and what he is up to, I want to know if anything happens at the time when it happens.

Leonardo was coming down slowly, with the information that he heard, he was slightly nervous, but not scared and to his people, he was strong as a pillar so even his eyes were trained to lie, hence nobody around him were able to make out that he was nervous.

He walked towards his room at least now he knows something. He knew that he is not searching in the dark.

The time is 10:30 PM. He spread out his bedroom took a hot water shower and after a good 72 hours, he hit the bed to find more or less rest.

20

Memories of yesterday will haunt you in the future. He called back as he essayed to catch some rest while holding on to his pillows. He could hear the outcries of all the people whose lineage, he has shed; but that didn't break him from what he is managing. He was behind money and feeling that he gets because of the power and the fright that the people get when they are face to face with him or even hearing his name; and the petty cries never bothered him. As a matter of fact, not even a drop of a tear roll down his nerves even when his father fell away, as he was expecting it and he really enjoyed the moment as he was next in line to assume charge of the family concern. His joy knew no bounds the day his father passed away.

But how can he, when he is responsible for his father's death, everybody thought about the fishiness that they smelt when Carunio Senior passed away, but they didn't spill the bean as it was Leonardo who was in front of them. Not a word of gossip even between the maids.

Ruthless son I'm he thought as he switched on the music because trying to get some sleep has become a distant dream for him. He didn't want to stop them, because even though he is ruthless, he would make sure that the next to kin is well aware of the whereabouts of the missing person, but definitely not with the help of the law, because not everyone is in his payrolls. There are efficient and competent police officers that he accepted to take care of, but with one person getting out of the way, he always had another two to worry most.

Corruption, would work, but not constantly. He popped a couple of tablets into his mouth, washed his face and tried to get some sleep and he was sure that within minutes that the sleeping pills he had would take effect.

Even after half an hour, he was agitated and was not able to produce the answer he desired. He woke up and popped another two pills and had a glass of milk that was there on the table.

He kept remaking the death scene of his father mentally over and over again; just to make sure that there were no witnesses and no loose ends. He always made sure that he did a thorough job. He constantly made certain that he got the mark of God invisible to the eyes of the jurisprudence, but he is not always successful as there would be people in every office who are slightly stupid and not perfectionists and he accepted to accept the blame for certain girls here and on that point even though he made certain that all his masses are well protected until and unless he obtain it otherwise.

The drug slowly started to get its effect.

The darkness slowly started to come down on his eyes as his eyelids began to shut down and he got into a mysterious slumber.

21

Don't underestimate Kevin, his connections are in big offices and we would need that sooner or later. And furthermore, he is rich as well, we are carrying green, but sometimes, there are spots where we would be required to swipe a card and his card won't be in the tracking list and more than that, his experience and intelligence does matter. Ambra could see the confidence on Brandon's face and she could read it loud and clear, that Brandon is saying, he would be a valuable asset in this case. And furthermore, who is capable to help us to a greater extent than the detective who investigated this event in the first place.

Kevin is kind a flirt and yes, sometimes he would be a botheration in the wrong spot. But his experience and his associations are much more significant than what we ask at this fourth dimension. You never know that probably we are in the most deadly fugitive list by now; Kevin would be our savior in this case, he would be an asset more than we can imagine at this point of time.

And more over, let's start our journey from where he stopped.

What about the tickets, we have booked only two, Ambra asked in confusion.

Cancel it and let me worry about our transportation Kevin said with a grin. Never underestimate the power of rich brat with connections.

He dialed a number which he has stored in his speed dial list and moved away to the deck where he talked. He disconnected the line and said we do not have much time, we need to scram to the Airport in the next one hour and we are fleeing to Brazil in the succeeding two hours, I have fixed up a private jet in my name and to avoid all suspicion, I said I'm flying with my beloved and her dad so act accordingly.

Brandon and Ambra looked at each other and smiled, while Kevin moved to pack his belongings that are required for him during this trip. He never forgets few things that he is needed to carry. He packed his Alfa Defender 9×19mm Parabellum and he knew that Brandon would be stuffed himself, but to be on the safe side, he also packed his Beretta 21 Bobcat, he knew if a time arrives, he could pitch it to Ambra, but not right away, he got hold of his suitcase, his laptop and other relevant things that he believed might be needed for his journey.

He had a reason why he didn't fling the gun at that period of time to Ambra. Both Kevin and Brandon had enough and more training both off and on the job, but Ambra, she might have not discovered a torpedo in her life as of today or so he thought. So this is not the right time to toss the gun to her and give her a fright.

Along with the bags, all of them disembarked from his yacht. Kevin whistled and a car with a chauffeur arrived; they all got into the car and Kevin just said Airport please.

At the airport, there were few young and beautiful ladies welcoming them and the ladies had all the papers to allow them inside the airport and immigration procedure was served promptly and there were no specific security checks because of the influence that Kevin had and more over they are leasing a private jet all the way from America to Brazil.

Thither was a car waiting for him to get them to the aircraft. As Kevin was welcomed again inside the aircraft by his beautiful crew, he winked at them, gave them a smile and walked in. This is an amazing flying machine said Ambra with all the latest gadgets attached to it; from WI-Fi to bean bag bucket seats and a good bar. Kevin smiled and they were headed towards their seats and were required to buckle their seat belts.

As shortly as the seat belt sign was switched off, Kevin got his laptop and switched it on, he loaded the files from Brazil to make him familiarize where he left the case and the people he interrogated. Ambra got up and walked towards the bar and asked for a double martini, while Brandon also took his laptop sat next to Kevin and they started their conversation and planning.

They were using codes and jargons, which Ambra was not able to follow; she didn't interrupt at that point of time as she knew they need to be on the same page when it comes to handling any situation that might arise on the way forward.

Kevin said I'm positive that he went to take a dirt nap in Turkey, so says my resources. How reliable are they? Well, thus far I've depended on them throughout my investigation career. They were always reliable. They are not police, they are former CIA secret agents and sources are substantial.

For a moment Brandon was shell shocked and Ambra could read his face, she inquired, is there something that I have to know? He said none at this point of time. If there is anything we would tell you. This is not going to work without communication. You are withholding information. If we are, then there would be a reason and those reasons are going to save you some times and at times we may be wrong as well, but there are decisions that we would have to take at certain times; Ambra please, never underestimate our decisions calls. Yes! Captain, Ambra said and those were the words coming out of an immature individual who is not convinced in whatever was said.

Ambra, first of all this is a deadly mission, we are stating that because we don't know what the effect of this would be. Probably finding your father would be the least important by the time we finish this. And this would be deadly.

Do you call up the map that we found on your dad's computer, God alone knows how many people are after that and where this is failing to pass us. We don't know, so everything at this point of time is calculations. We would have to work out on all permutations and combinations. This is to make certain that all of us survive and without any damage that we would be able to revert to our normal lives.

Brandon stood up and kept his hand on her shoulder, turned her and in a lower voice he said you have to trust us, we are going to be with you in every step of the way and there is no turning back. We will find your father, probably not in the way that you expect, but we will find the truth.

Kevin could see the concern in Brandon's voice. He just moved to the bar and ordered my regular, Cassandra. She smiled and served his drink. He went straight to Brandon, took his arm and pulled him into another seat in that airplane and where Ambra wouldn't be able to ear-drop. I have been round the block a million times, only she is not your case; I'm dying to attempt.

Brandon just smiled

22

Leonardo and Amy were walking along a beach. For Leonardo, Amy was a girl whom he could tell everything, more than a love of his life, he cared and always wanted to be by her side; the romantic avatar of the most atrocious person.

Amy, who moved to the city with dreams of being a fashion designer and to open her own fashion boutique; met Leonardo in a fashion meeting where Leonardo was invited; initially, she was not willing to give in, but for her, she wanted a support in the new place and Leonardo has been just a stepping stone to her success. A man with money looks and fame. He had all that she wanted to be successful in life; but as she talked to him and she came to know more about him, she slowly started to give in. So she used to be with Leonardo whenever he wanted to let the cat out of the bag.

Today is one such day.

Leonardo was talking about that piece of paper that was handed down his generations and due to his careless mistake he lost it. And the hunt is on for that piece of paper or cloth I'm not even sure what it is. She asked in curiosity, what is the content in that paper or the material that you lost? I'm not sure and I didn't care. I didn't take a second look at that piece of paper before I handed it to my most trusted man. For me the value was that, it was handed down through my generations like a family heirloom. Nothing more, nothing less; it is more than 2000 or more years old which makes it the most unique and a priceless artifact.

I kill people and my associates have killed people, in order to recover it but were in vain. Before long I'll throw my hands on that, the hunt is on. Not sure where it is going to lead me, but the hunt for that is on.

She embraced him and sounded out, don't worry, I'm there by your side and I'll be there. You will find it, I have faith in you and I know you. Don't get frustrated, we will sail through this phase smoother than you can expect.

He smiled and kept her close as they go on their walk.

Amy grinned and she said it's been a while since you asked me out for dinner and fetched me something. He said let everything settle first and then we will go to Paris and celebrate until then be with me. She didn't state anything as you could see clearly in her eyes that her intention was something else. She was a master of emotions and she very well knew how to conceal them in plain view.

He got a call on his cell phone. He stated, I got to do this.

The richest guy in the world using an old school phone, Amy was baffled. He resolved the call with Amy next to him and she could overhear the conversation subtly and the other person said we were tracking Brandon's passport, he simply departed the country on a private jet that is scheduled to make it here in Brazil this evening. We can keep an eye from the airport.

What time is the flight landing? 4:30PM. Good, I want to be in the airport while the flight lands and I want to see this person. I think he doesn't know that hell is watching over him wherever he passes away and it's simply a matter of time before I hug him to end. And that day, he would understand the phrase that Hell has broken loose.

Post his conversation, she asked. Why use an old school phone. I can tell you the secret, but I would have to kill you. Her face lowered.

He just laughed out loud; there is no big secret in this. You know that a lot of people who upholds the law are behind me. If I start using the phones that you people call smart which are available in the market today, I would be cornered easily. The phone today comes with a GPS tracker and they would be able to close in on my location where ever I travel. I'm very secure here in Brazil like a youngster who is safe on his mother's laps. But the moment I step out of the country, you will never know when they will cover me. On this phone, I do not have GPS, and their best bet is to triangulate the signals from the closest three towers and try to zero in on my spot and I just need that time to find away from where I'm to where I want to be, which makes me harder to seize.

I may not be the smartest person on earth, but I'm definitely not stupid.

But Yes! This phone can be tracked by my people only and only they know how.

23

The plane started to descend and was minutes away from a touchdown. Brandon tossed a passport to Ambra and said from this moment on you are not Ambra Gallo, you would be the address as Ms Camila Levoff and I would be Fabio Diaz. She looked at the passport and was didn't understand the reason, it was her photograph on a Brazilian Passport. Memorize our names and we might require it when we go through the immigration.

Kevin said we don't have a clue if anyone is behind us, if there is someone, then in that case, we don't want them to track our whereabouts; simple.

Ambra nodded her head in agreement and she kept saying her new name in her head a hundred times, so she would respond to them if they call her new name.

Cassandra, Kevin called, give her a new hair color and a new hairdo, they shouldn't be able to narrow her down to a facial recognition software. Brandon opened the door of the washroom and for a moment with this new look, she was surprised to see a new figure on that plane, she turned to Kevin for an answer; he could read her face, who the hell is he?

Brandon, came out of the room with a new look, he had put a fake tummy, white beard and a mole on the forehead and to give it a final touch a new dental work as well. He was ready to be dashed by any camera and it would take days, before the facial recognition tool to cast his real identity, certain tips and tricks that he learned back in the force.

After a few minutes, the seat belt sign was turned on.

As they were walking out of the plane, Leonardo was waiting outside the airport looking for them and was dying to see them. He was connected on his phone with his team back home and the minute their passports are entered he would know.

Camila, Fabio shouted, this way please. They swiped their passports through the gates of immigration and the board read "Returning Citizens" without much hassle the door was opened and they were on the other side of the counter and they waited for Kevin. Brandon had a walking stick in his hand; very slowly they moved to the belt where their baggages were arriving after the security check. And with Kevin's influence, all the baggage's came in without any security issues even though there were weapons packed inside it.

They passed Leonardo right under his nose and he was not able to recognize them nor did anyone confirm that they walked out.

What the hell just happened? All the passengers who came in a private jet and other passengers who landed around the same time departed the airport and they didn't make it, is that what you are reading. The private jet that was scheduled to reach Brazil has landed; but neither our facial recognition tool nor the immigration counter made an entrance. We were not able to zero in on them.

Eventually he calmed down. They are smart and I need to be smarter in order to get to them I need to start thinking

They might have passed by me and yet I was not able to identify them. As he was thinking this, they were actually boarding the car right behind him, which took them to a hotel where they would be staying.

Kevin made the entry and paid using his credit card and they moved to their new location. As soon as they got into their rooms, Brandon and Kevin the computers were set up and started their search afresh.

If we are to find out why he departed to Turkey and what occurred, we need to revive the whole incidents that led him thither.

As per the details what Ambra has provided us, from the recording of those voicemails, letter and from the map that was found on his computer, let's follow it backwards.

Post changing their looks they started off by exploring the net for the incident that took place. And from an anonymous blog they read the whole thing about the killing in broad daytime and the police and the hooligans helping Leonardo to wash off a crime scene more professionally that they CSU's.

They ran the name of Leonardo in all possible databases including Google to find an answer and it was there in front of them in no time.

Everything, every single detail about Leonardo from various databases and more importantly, that he was flagged as a wanted terrorist by the Interpol, FBI, CIA everybody. They look at each other and said unanimously "We have a challenge."

24

This blog doesn't have the whereabouts of the witnesses and this blog has been updated from a ghost account. Probably, the person updated this blog is scared that someone might come behind him. As a witness to a major crime like this; if this Leonardo is behind all this mess, he ought to be.

They had everything in front of them about Leonardo. His picture, his fingerprints, his DNA, last known address, list of known associates, everything what they wanted to know about Leonardo. Brandon and Kevin were looking at the photographs of all the known associates and together they pointed their finger at one associate and said let's start with this one. He looks like the type who would break easily.

Ambra sitting on the bed stated what you are here for, to catch Leonardo or to find my father. To find your father and what he was up to - an immediate response from Bandon. From the time we started re-looking into your father's case, Leonardo's name has been popping up not once but in multiple places. We can't talk directly to him, but we need a short swing to get to him and that would be this bugger and we have our doubts to believe that he might be behind all this. And we need to understand what it is. And I would recommend that you don't follow us when we try to capture this guy, as Kevin is a master of torture and he would get the information by hook or crook. Hence it's better you stay out of this. No way said Ambra, I wanted to hear everything he has to say and about the torture, I won't look, but I want answers straight from the horse's mouth.

If you insist, but to get to him, we need to know what he does on a daily basis, his routine and how and where we can nab him. This city has two types of surveillance, one to make sure that the city is safe or their citizens and tourists and the second is Leonardo's, making sure that everything is running as per his plan. I'm sure that Leonardo's team is watching this city and we need to dress up again and we cannot grant him any doubt nor should be seen on camera. I have a gut feeling that he was preying for us outside the airport, if that is true, then he would be thinking that we are smarter than him and he would be formulating a plan to get better of us and we shouldn't give any room for that. And he will try to be smarter, but how I don't know. We need to stay ahead of him at all times and we don't have what he has. Time and men; he doesn't have what we have, two brains, amalgamation of cop and criminal brains and a beauty. Ambra just smiled and then she reacted, what, I don't have brains is that what you are saying. No, what we implied is that you don't have the combat kind of experience and the brain that we referred to is the last minute decision making capabilities. And do you know, what is the foremost thing that we would be trained on before we head out for a combat? What? Ambra was not inquisitive. "We all go home" They ask us to say this aloud a hundred times before we start any trainings or before we head into the war zone. We all go home. So remember that and keep saying that in your mind Camila. You would need it.

That is definitely a good thing. "We all go home" and whatever happens, keep that in the back of your mind. Camila, always remember; never get caught, because the hunter would become the hunted. Leonardo and his team are experts in torturing and killing. So its better we stay a little away from him. Whatever happens – and Ambra completed – WE ALL GO HOME.

You wanted to be part of it, right. Tomorrow morning you need to sit in the coffee shop behind this hotel. Note: you would be alone in this mission; this man would be coming there and would be asking for his regular espresso. From that moment on, I want him to be followed, the best way to follow a man is making him follow you and the rest would be history, especially when we are not looking for his hideout but we want to lure him to ours. The reason why I'm saying this is because, if he starts to follow you the people watching the live CCTV footage, would think that he is making a move rather than alerting them a woman is following one of theirs. Hence be careful, you necessitate to make believe that he is following you or you two are together. Whatever happens, you do not follow him. If not today, we will do it tomorrow, but never run behind him seeking attention and he would be alarmed. It is imperative that you heed to us. The earlier the better, but at the same time, I would say, safer the better. If not today, we always have a tomorrow, said Kevin.

You need to deceive him. He needs to infer that you are local as if you are from a nearby town came to discover the major metropolis. Which means you need to be a local tourist confused in this big city; you would be wired at all times. We will hear what you hear and we will see what you see. We are also going to give you an eye in the back as well just in case to make sure that we are safe and in case you need to run, you need to run. Trust us when you are down there and you obey everything we say without any doubt, if we say duck, you duck; if we ask you to run, you run; when you are running, we ask you to take a left and then duck, do that. Trust us without questioning. Are we all clear?

Yes! Fabio, Crystal.

Here is what we know about him; probably this information is something that might save you. Information that we are disclosing is to help you; which means, all these information are on need to know basis, no questions further.

He enjoys his morning espresso without sugar- that raw taste of coffee is what he wishes. He is a movie buff and has got a weakness towards hookers. He is soft with them and nasty to others. He won't be a tough nut to crack.

For the last time, do not follow him, make him follow you and have him pursue you. And if that is the case, this is the map of Brazil, this is where we want him and we will do our bit of work. You lead him there and we take care of the rest. Now Camila, what happens when you trust us, she smiled and said "WE ALL GO HOME"

25

We all go home, kept lingering in her head as she was waiting in the coffee shop, she was too dressed for the occasion so that to make sure that she catches an eye, the eye of the person that she desires. She was feeling good as she is now a sole participant of this adventure and she knew that to an extend she is safe as there are eyes on her and she has a two way conversation system camouflaged on her dress.

A waitress came near her and said - Posso pegar seu pedido, por favor (May I take your order, please). Brandon and Kevin heard this through the speakers and looked at each other. This is something we overlooked, the language. Brazilians speak Portuguese; what do we do? Brandon took the microphone hurriedly to provide her with the correct reply.

Sim, por favor, gostaria de ter um pequeno-almoço Americano (Yes, Please I would like to have an

American breakfast) Sim senhora (Yes madam) and she left.

I didn't know you speak Portuguese, Brandon said over the microphone. She took the newspaper and covered her face to be careful just in case if someone is watching. There are lots of things that you don't know about me. No worries, you will get used to it and there would be a lot of opportunities for you to learn.

Kevin just masked his smile, while Brandon looked at him after hearing her reply.

Subject at 10 O'clock, she heard through the earpiece.

The waitress served her some sausages, bread and a coffee. She just nodded her head as if she is saying Thank you.

The man gave her a look and went inside and she could see that he is talking to the waitress and giving her a look. She was cautious enough not to give him a second look and she was enjoying the view. He was also conscious of her speed in which she is eating her breakfast. She cannot be too fast as if she is in a hurry nor can be very slow as if she had all the time in the world. In order to adjust her timing, she opened her bag and took out a book and started to read through the pages, which gave her ample time to finish her breakfast and to complete her mission. She was hoping that he would start the conversation. And within no time her prayer was answered. He came to her Olá, SIM Olá she responded Você não está a partir desta parte DA cidade você está? (You are not from this part of town, are you?) Não, eu venho de uma aldeia próxima, mas foi criado na América (No, I come from a village nearby, but was raised in the America) With a very heavy Portuguese slang he said no wonder your language is a little rusty. She smiled and tried to put on an accent. For a very long time I was in the United States of America, but now I had this dream of coming to Brazil to see the place where my parents were born. I stay with my grandma in a nearby village. Ah! So I can tell you are a tourist. Absolutely, for the time being and actually I'm a tourist, visiting this place for the first time.

What do you do? Business… mainly. Do you dine here often? Yes! I come here every day. I always start my day with a coffee and I like it here and this is close by to my workplace. That's nice. Anyways, nice to meet you, probably we will see each other around sometime, that too if I'm here tomorrow. Been in Brazil for a week and I was planning to head back to my village by evening. And Ambra stood up and actioned for the check. The waitress brought the check and she gave a credit card.

Brandon, what a blunder is she doing, I have told her explicitly that she cannot use her credit card and still she had the audacity to do it. She heard the comment, but didn't respond as she was not in a situation to do so.

She signed the receipt and she left waving him goodbye.

What is she doing now? Kevin said wait Brandon, I think I understand what she is doing and you have a lot to learn about women. Bro, you need to come out of your hiding and start seeing people and if you had, you wouldn't have made that comment. I'm sure that you still read the magazines on Paleontology and trying to get up to date with the new weapons and their usage. You are still old school man and very predictable. You need to and I mean when I say this, you need to come out of your hiding and start seeing people. Now watch, she is a real pro in doing this.

She heard that comment too; she smiled as she was walking towards the hotel. She was not too fast and not too slow. The man was thinking behind her and she was careful enough not to turn around and give him a second look.

He stood there confused what to do? Without wasting much time, he ran behind her and caught up with her. Hey! You again, she said. Yeah! I'm sorry I didn't catch your name, I'm Camila and you are, Marcos, you can call me Marc. Well, nice to meet you Marc. Actually, I too have to walk this path, so I was guessing we could divvy up the route together. She smiled at his comment. Sure, why not.

So where do you work? A couple of blocks from here its close by. No worries and I have some time to spend. Actually, loads of time, if you are free. Considerably, as a matter of fact, I have visited this place and was getting rather lonely. Probably there are places that I haven't seen before and would you be kind enough to show your neighborhood? Why not?

In that case, come with me to the hotel, I need to get my camera and my bag. And so we will maneuver out and explore the places that I haven't experienced before.

He was tickled, he thought am I an expert now or am I getting lucky.

This way to the hotel, Camila; Yes, I know Marc, just need to buy something from that shop around that corner and then we will head there.

Sure!

It was the queue for Brandon and Kevin to head down and wait; as she is luring him to the alley where they can nab him.

26

As the darkness of the alley closed upon him, he warned Camila, it's not safe to be here even in broad daylight. Did you know that there is a shop right around that corner that sells antiques? I was there last evening and I didn't have enough money and he didn't accept credit cards. And moreover, why should I be scared when you are there with me? Shouldn't I be feeling safe? He just smiled and walked along with her.

As they turned around the corner, Brandon and Kevin jumped in front of him and sprayed the concentrated version of chloroform on his face.

Three hours later, he woke up tied to an iron chair that is nailed to the ground, as if the place is ready for them to do anything. He looked around and was not able to find anyone there. The place was shady, kind of dark with a filthy odor. He could feel things moving round his feet, but was not able to scare it away, as his legs were also drawn and he could barely run. He was still in a sleepy state of mind as he has not gained his consciousness completely.

He closed his eyes and took a deep breath and shouted - Me Free bastardos (Free me bastards) CAMILA, he shouted.

Brandon and Kevin came towards him and they have instructed Ambra to watch from a distance and make sure that you are out of sight for Marc. He shouldn't be able to see you.

Americanos – Brandon smiled Qual é o problema com os americanos (What's the problem with Americans). You want to know the problem you jerk. The problem with American's is that, they have a lot of issues within their country and still they want to poke their nose into what others do. Americans are not the world police, why don't you stick to your country and stop bothering others. You should be ashamed of yourself, you think you are praised everywhere, but the fact still remains the same, that you are just poking your nose for unnecessary things and people are talking behind your back and they hate you.

He has a point there. Well, now we see why you hate Americans. But do you think we took all the trouble and brought you here to hear this. You are thoroughly mistaken Marco. How do you know my name? Yes! Where is Camila? Did you kill her?

That is none of your business, Marco. You should be concerned about your life and not hers. We are working to give you an opportunity to outlast, to endure your life the way you want to. But you would have to answer a couple of questions for us. And we will let you go scot-free

Alright! Are you ready to co-operate with us?

Yes! Ask me what you want to know.

They took a photograph of Leonardo, who is he?

He is Leonardo Carunio; the last living member of the Carunio mafia clan.

Wow! That was a truth and pretty good for a start.

Why was he at the airport yesterday? Kevin just thought that might be relevant, but didn't know that he would get an answer.

There has to be some reason if he was at the airport not all in his team would know the reason. He just thought, if it clicks, he won't be searching for a needle in a haystack.

I don't know why he was there at the airport, if he was, he would have a reason.

Seriously! You are going to give us that answer.

I don't know. I seriously don't know. I'm a junior in his tribe. If he was indeed in the airport, you should be talking to other people in his team. I'm not the right guy, I have been with Leonardo for a year now and I'm not one of the most trusted people that he has with him. Unlike cops, they do know how to keep a secret. I don't know. There are cops who are corrupted and who are not. We don't have two kinds, we have one kind. The name of that kind is Loyal, so I'm telling you; it would be very hard for you to get information from any of us.

Alright! Enough of your speech, who do you reckon we should bring into question to obtain the right results?

Steve would be the very best person to get the answers for you. Kevin smiled and said you are going to get him here for us. In the very same alley and we would let you know. And from the alley, we take care.

Kevin dragged Camila to him. You want to see her alive, you better hurry, if the time exceeds my friend she would be gone and you would be responsible. And our men are already in your house, one wrong move you can also kiss your family goodbye.

You can talk to them alright, but not now, once the mission is complete. And you know what will happen to your family, if things go wrong.

Don't say that. You have 30 minutes to get him here; Kevin untied the ropes he had on him. 30 minutes on my watch and gave a phone to him that can be traced and they would be able to listen to all the calls that he gets and he does.

He ran out, he tried calling his home number, none answered the minute he made that call, they routed that number to Brandon's cell phone without him knowing about it and to him, his wife didn't answer the call, which made him panic.

The second call was made to Steve. The phone went ringing for a very long time and just before it was about to get disconnected, the call was answered.

Hi! This is Steve.

27

This is Marco. Marco? Who? Marco A143 – To identify everyone in the team, Leonardo has given each of them a number and that's how they would identify each other, even in case if someone is in trouble, number helps identify them. And these numbers would be tattooed on their arm, beneath the armpit, just to make sure that is not easily visible, but would be able to identify themselves when in trouble and if found dead.

Yes! Marco, how can I help you? Would you be able to come to the corner of Wordsworth Library?

You mean that dark alley, Marco? What are you doing there and what kind of trouble have you created? I will explain this in detail when you reach here. How soon do you think you would be able to reach? Depending on the traffic and the place that I'm in right now, I might take an hour to reach. Can't you reach early? I will start now and let's see how soon I can reach. Ok! And the line got disconnected.

Brandon and Kevin have already triangulated to the signals and have narrowed down their search to understand the present location of Steve and moreover, they remotely switched on the GPS tracker on the phone in-order for them to get a live feed on what he is doing.

They were able to see that he is driving an old car and was traveling at a speed of 40 miles per hour through an open road. And they were anticipating his visit at any time. In-order to raise no suspicion, Brandon called Marco asking for the status. He needs an hour to reach. But our agreement was within 30 minutes. Please, I beg you, give me an hour and I would get you Steve as promised, but I need more time.

Agreed, now you are left with 45 minutes, let's see, who wins.

Now they have a face to go with for Steve, as they downloaded a clear image while they were watching the live feed.

They exactly knew where Steve is and how he is going to arrive and they have already masterminded the entire plan how they are going to interrogate him.

He parked his car in one corner and started walking towards the alley where Marco waved him just to show where he is standing and Steve signaled him back inquiring about what happened and why called suddenly. He was more interested to know what kind of trouble that Marco fall into, on the way to Marco, he unlocked his leather and kept in weapon in ready position; all set to draw if need be.

Brandon was watching this through a binocular through his hotel window and Kevin was going down to settle the man. He knew that he had to create a scene behind the alley in order to get the unbiased attention from Steve.

He took Marco by his collar and pulled into the shed where he was held captive. Seeing this Steve started to run through the alley and got into a shed just to see him alone there and he was not able to figure out where Marco is and the guy who pulled Marco inside. He got confused and was thinking to himself, what kind of trouble this guy fall into. He drew his gun from the leather and loaded the weapon just to make sure. And started to search for him frantically and started calling his name.

Unexpectedly a black cloth covered his face and someone took the gun from his hand, handcuffed him and dragged him. He knew nobody was out there to hear him scream.

They took him by hand, made him sit on a chair, where he was tied tightly against it and was hardly any room for him to move around and from the feel of it, he knew that was an iron chair and he sat there unable to do anything.

The black cloth that covered his face was removed and he could see Marco tied to another chair in another corner of the room.

Steve asked them, what is that you want? And why did you bring us here?

In the meantime, Brandon was searching his pockets, don't tickle me man, tell me what you want or you are going to regret that you did this. Brandon, without changing his face and without uttering a word to him, continued his search.

Took the phone from his jacket pocket, switched off the GPS and removed the battery and tossed it to Kevin and said strip. Kevin stripped the entire phone and then connected it to his computer for existing data download from the phone.

Steve was watching all this. Tell me what you want as if he started to lose his patience. Brandon shouted, there is absolutely no reason why you should shout or lose your patience. We will take our time and we will ask you what we want to know and you would give us what we are looking for and more over my friend you would be as good as dead, if you don't co-operate. So for the time being, until we are ready, patience is the virtue.

Steve didn't talk after that. He waited patiently until they returned the next morning.

Marco's mouth was taped so that he can't let the cat out of the bag and his hands and legs were also tied so that he couldn't signal Steve on what's occurring.

Even if Marco wanted to say something, Steve didn't allow as Steve was having his head held down and was thinking what do they want to know and how he should strategize the answers and get away quick. He wanted to get back to Leonardo and tell him what happened. He also thought what kind of blackmails or tortures are they going to use against him to put away with things he knew. According to him, they were some agency trying to capture Leonardo, the place was dim and he was not able to see their faces clearly. And if he did, he would have recognized Brandon and would have anticipated the questions and answers that he is going to provide.

He didn't sleep that night, he wanted to remain that way, whatever happens and all he could think about was an escape plan from the place where he is held captive.

Marco on the other hand was making sounds to get his attention and from the place where Steve is sitting to see Marco clearly was not possible, too much haze and smokes in the room and to add it to the glory it was kind of dark too.

The three amigos were watching them through the camera that they have placed in the basement of that building. And they had motion sensors and at the same time audio, just in case that they try to escape.

They wanted to escape, but they were not in the right frame of mind to do so. Half sedated, tied to an iron chair with no possible means of communication and more they have no idea where they are.

Kevin's computer beeped and it was time for them to look into the phone records. Multiple calls from an unknown number, all these calls lasted less than five seconds. In today's world, getting a marketing call is not unusual, most of us just disconnect the call, Ambra said. But both Brandon and Kevin didn't let that go, we need to trace that number. Why are you wasting your time boys? No Ambra, this is not just a marketing call. Look at the time difference from one call to another – less than 4 hours. The calls have originated from the same location and the pattern, one call exactly every four fours, this is no marketing call, this is real. We need to trace that number and now we know that we have less than 5 seconds to catch whoever is making this call, the only possibility of a search is, we need to listen into that call otherwise we need one minute to hack the number. We will figure that out.

Let's look at the images from his memory card and from his phone memory. The majority of the photos are unfamiliar, and lots of different places, guess he has taken these pictures over a very long period and had no patience to download it. It is difficult to narrow down on the search to find out where this place belongs. Even the geographical location software that can predict the place using the landmarks and other details on this image; but that is a long shot and would take a lot of time to understand these locations, but do we need that is that question. And I guess not, said Brandon.

Guys let me remind you this, we are here for my father and what does this guy Leonardo or anyone matters here.

Did you forget the blog about the accident that your father mentioned and moreover we are being followed.

Ambra was shell shocked to hear that, Leonardo or his team murdered a man in broad daylight and no action has been taken against him. He is a wanted person by different departments and now we are being followed, she was trying to connect the dots. You don't think my father is….

That is a possibility, said Kevin. That's what I try to put into your head while you were at my yacht and you didn't want to believe. From this very moment, you need to anticipate that and keep that idea in the back of your head. If it's confirmed, you would have the boldness to face that; if it's vice versa, then you can consider it a bonus and a new life.

Let's put a bug in his phone so that we can listen to phone calls and track the signal if need be. Good idea, Brandon stated Kevin.

Now comes the most important part of the phone, Text messages. There was only one message from a number – that read – "Package Arrived"

28

Disappointed from the airport, Leonardo moved to his favorite hotel, the shabbiest one on the route. He wanted to rejuvenate himself and that was the place he knew. From dealers of all kinds, homeless people, and people looking for fun and hookers were the people who actually stayed there and people who made money from these poor souls by the act of serving them, are they actually served? A question, that people demand when they ante up the money for the hour or for the night at the cashier's desk.

But for Leonardo the services were different, he could get anything that he wants and also is capable of getting away from places others think as impossible. That was the power of the money and fright that the people had for him and the hooligans around him.

Tonight was the kind of night that every police department wanted, he was alone, away from his bodyguards and he was also away from home. But unfortunately, nobody knows and the people who knew kept their mouths shut.

As he walked in, the lady at the counter just handed over a key and said 201. He nodded and walked past the counter. She took the register and wrote Super Man.

He opened the door, the bed was neatly kept, and the washroom was shabby, but of course it was dry. There was a table in the corner and pad, pen and a lamp on the table. No TV, No internet, no phone, made the place beautiful, he wanted to get away from the world. And again, why do you need all this, especially when you rent for an hour or two?

Wanted some time to think about the events and wanted to see if he could find a way to understand and learn how to get closer to Brandon, he wanted a rendezvous, he knew he would get that sooner or later, but now, how can I stop them, what are they looking for? A set of questions that was lingering need answers and he wanted to be at peace.

He shut the door and was walking to the bed, to loosen up and re-produce the entire events to fetch something out of that.

As he was walking towards his bed, he heard a knock on the door; he turned back and took a long breath. He walked towards the door and opened it; there she was standing, tall, slim and beautiful. You could have me for 200 USD. He smiled and said you and your friends knock on this door again, I would have to pay 200 USD to wipe your face off my floor. She was taken aback; none so far has come in such a force against her. Sorry, she said and ran. He slammed the door shut again.

He moved the bed and kept it close to the window, where he could see the world outside through his window. He kept the pillow in a straight position and leaned back on the pillow, staring outside.

He analyzed one event at a time and he went back all the way to the time, where his father handed him the paper that was passed down as a family legacy. He handed the letter to the person whom he trusted the most, he got a phone call at that point of time and he looked worried and he was hurried outside without wasting much time.

Haste makes waste, he thought to himself, he was not running to sell that or to dupe him, he was running to take care of something else. I shouldn't have taken a decision like the one I took and I guess that ignited the entire series of events.

I got upset and sent some of my people behind him and he understood that I thought he did something wrong. He could have surrendered and told me the whole story, but with that being said I was not the kind of guy who would listen, I live on perceptions, like a lot of people around me, everywhere, in every organization, the boss creates a perception about their employees and would live with that. And a boss like that is always the hardest to crack. Whatever you do, you have not done enough, small mistakes you pay with your life. You would be demoralized to work and you would be out of confidence and out of motivation. I'm such a boss, the people who work for me are not working because, they like me, it's because they are scared and at the end of the day, the world is for the survivors only and only the fittest shall survive.

He wanted to survive and I was not a good listener, he knew that and so he ran, ran for his life. And he was misunderstood. They chased him and before he rode the pale horse, he slipped the paper into someone else.

And it took a great deal of manpower and money to clear the mess that my people had made in broad daylight. Keeping it out of the media and keeping it away from public and more over making it look like an accident in the police report. Couldn't have managed without the fear they had against me. This is me and I cannot change, it would be a great deal for me to change, but as a matter of fact, if I change, I won't be me anymore and I cannot live with that.

He slipped the paper into someone else, who was nowhere related to me, just a tourist and it took a lot of time for me to hunt him down and I just asked my people to wait for my orders and keep him under tight surveillance all the time.

We were keeping him on a tight surveillance, but he managed to give us a slip and we got him back on our network when he reached Turkey, why? Is it that piece of paper through brought him to Turkey? If so, what was in that paper?

Brandon, how did he get involved with Ambra? Why is he helping her? Who is he? What are they looking for? Few more questions, he wanted an answer to and then everything would be crystal clear or so he thought.

If that is the old paper that brought him to Turkey and I guess it's him that brought Ambra and Brandon to Brazil. They won't find him here, he was killed in Turkey and my paper that was old and it was burned to ashes, so either he made a copy of that paper, but again, they should be going to Turkey if so, but why in Brazil?

Leonardo, kept connecting the dots the whole night, but he was not able to put the entire story together, there were many pieces of the puzzle missing to complete the entire story. And that's what kept him awake, till the sun came out of its hiding place and sent the moon into hiding.

He got up from bed, washed his face and as he was wiping the water off his face He heard another knock on his door, he opened it and was surprised to see Amy there. What are you doing in this place? She asked. How did you find me, he wanted to know that first.

She smiled and said sweetheart, what is bothering you? How did you find me? She could hear the harshness in his tone and she knew this is not that moment to beat around the bush. It was easy finding you here, the girl that you scared away last night is a friend of mine. She recognized you from the pictures that I had and she informed me that you were here. He showed a sign of relief.

So again, what is bothering you?

He said nothing, as he moved from the door, showing her that she was welcome.

29

We cannot trace that number, that message was sent to a burner phone and only he would know, who had that phone at the time when he sent that message.

So is it time?

Time for what, Ambra asked.

Kevin and Brandon looked at each and smiled. She didn't understand the joke, but she played along as if she understood the meaning of that. Guys, time to get some squeaks.

She just followed them and they reached the basement of the hotel where they stayed and the sole reason why they took that hotel is because of that unused basement. Brandon knew about it, it was once the MI secret hideout, and they had almost all their equipments loaded, but today, it's just a basement that many doesn't know about it.

That is one of the reasons why Marco and Steve doesn't know about this place or where they are. When they woke up from their sedation, they were here.

They signaled Ambra to be slightly away from this and this would be a little for her to digest. She obliged, she wanted to see what they are going to do before she broke that rule of staying away.

To start with, what is your name? Brandon asked softly.

As if I would start talking, you might want to try harder and when we start trying harder, you cannot request us to be softer because the minute we start becoming softer, you wouldn't like it.

He just grinned.

Alright! Let's try this again, what is your name?

You should already know what my name is, yup! We know, said Kevin, but we wanted to make sure that you are the right person that we are looking for, else why do you want to take unnecessary beatings for a wrong man.

Ah! That's a sound direction to embark on; in that event, I'm Steve. Brandon and Kevin looked at each other, they understood, he is scared, but not that scared, he may sustain torture, but not for long, he would give up very soon and we don't have to try real hard.

What do you do? Business, the answer came as an immediate reply

That is very good, what kind of business? It's called none of your business.

Brandon took a screw driver and cut his palm in the center, Ambra could hear him scream from a distance and Marco was getting disturbed and scared.

What kind of business? Being in this line of work, I have experienced a lot and have gone through a great deal and this cute little thing that you just behaved, would not even constitute to 0.01% of what I have experienced.

I agree, being with Leonardo, you would have done and would have experienced a lot of things.

The mention of Leonardo's name caught his attention. Who are you? What do you want with me?

Too late in asking those questions my friend, you should have started with those questions rather than threatening us.

What kind of business? None of your business was the reply again. Kevin took a lighter and lit the fire under the small finger on his right hand. Now I can move this heat towards your index finger, but with a change, I will use the welding machine to do it and you can feel your fingers melt right behind you.

All types of business, all types including armory distribution globally to the needy, prostitution, gambling, smuggling and everything under the sun.

Why was Leonardo at the airport?

Who? Leonardo? Who is he?

This time, he chopped off a finger from Steve. You want to try again on that answer? I don't know any Leonardo, he cried in pain.

Brandon took a knuckle bar and started cracking one bone after another in his hand; I will keep doing this until I get an answer from you.

I don't know any Leonardo, seriously, I don't know him.

Alright!

They ripped his shirt and used a metal clip on his nipples and connected that to a wire, which ended up on a battery, do you know what will happen, if we connect this end to the battery.

He was looking for some Brandon. I don't know who he is.

Why Brandon? Don't know, he is helping some girl named Ambra Gallo. Her father had something that belonged to Leonardo. We tried to get that back from him but were in vain. We were never able to recover what was lost.

Where is her father now? Last seen in Turkey, Leonardo had some people following him and they lost him there, I don't know the rest of the story.

What is that thing that belonged to him and was with her father? Not sure, some paper he said that was passed on to him through generation.

Where did he get the information about Brandon and Ambra? I don't know

Wrong answer my friend. He connected the wire to the battery and the electricity passed through his body, while he cried in pain.

They stopped, you want to try that answer again, he slowly started going into a state of shock along with the sedation that he had on him. He was going to sleep. They used a tooth driller and started drilling his tooth and give him pain in his head to keep him alive.

They chopped his tiny fingers on his legs by an inch. He screamed in pain, we could torture you all day and I should admit this, I hadn't done this in a long time and I'm enjoying this.

Once more, from where or who passed information to Leonardo about Brandon and Ambra? He didn't say anything, they used a surgical blade to create wounds in different parts of the body and applied some fine alcohol on that and the sting got him singing.

He got the information about Ambra from the person who filed a missing persons information and about Brandon from a facial recognition software which he ran against the armed forces confirmed dead database.

But as soon as he saw his photograph on the screen, like a virus attack all the systems were down and we were not able to recover the details. Hence all he knows is how Brandon looks and he was in the armed forces. He knows nothing more and nothing less.

Where is he now? Not sure, he can be anywhere, he is usually at his home not far from where we met, it would be easy for you to identify the place, and all you got to do is travel towards the opposite road from where you captured us.

Brandon and Kevin looked at each other and nodded.

Kevin switched on the light at one corner and there was Marco tied to a chair, unhurt and all well.

Brandon said Thank you Marco for luring Steve to us.

And at that spot of time, Steve knew that he was betrayed and more over, Marco used him to get out unscathed.

They gave sedatives to both Steve and Marco, planted a bug on their phone, dressed them up and waited for dusk.

Later that night, they took both of them to a nearby beach tucked the phone in their pockets and left them there, they knew when the sedation is worn out, they would try to call the first person who can help them in this situation and if their luck is still there, it would be Leonardo.

30

When the power of the sedation was over, Steve woke up first and also discovered Marco along with him, his anger knew no bounds at that time seeing Marco unhurt, but he wanted to take that vendetta with Marco along with Leonardo. He was in a great deal of pain; he looked into his pouch and found his phone. He checked Marco's pockets as well and found his phone.

He knew that something was up, but unfortunately, he was not in the right state to move around and ask for help. He called Leonardo's number to ask for help.

Just as they expected, the number was traced and they were able to listen to the conversation.

Hey Leo, it's me Steve, I have been abducted and is in a lot of pain, can't talk straight, would help if you could use my signal to understand my position and send for help.

What do you mean by abducted, before he could reply Brandon disconnected that call remotely.

Leonardo's people were given the number to trace and they triangulated the signal and the help reached them in no time. They were picked up by his gang members, and they took him straight to Leonardo.

Leonardo had a look at both of them, Marco was still unconscious. Steve said I'm not sure who abducted me and they tortured me to speak the known facts about why you were at the airport and other details.

Did you tell them? I had to, I was in pain so bad, that I couldn't resist much longer.

How did they find you? They didn't, it was Marco, who helped them to lure me into their den. And what did Marco say? Not sure, whether he knew anything. He called me and said he was in trouble; asked me to meet him near the Words Worth Library and I don't remember how I landed up in their control, I was sedated and was tied to a chair.

Eventually, I had to give in.

Do you know the rules of the gang? Yes, I do.

What is it? Torture me, kill me, and kill my people. I will not betray the fraternity.

And what did you do? Steve was silent and kept his head low

Without wasting much time, Leonardo cleared his leather and before he knew it, he kissed the ground and his phone rolled out under the table nearby. Within minutes, his corpse was cleared and the area was cleaned.

What do we do about Marco? Let him come to his senses and then we will think about it, Leonardo said.

Leonardo turned towards the monitor and Marco slowly started to wake up.

Brandon and Kevin – Now that we have traced his number, could we triangulate his location, Kevin asked. You are the computer expert, what do you say? We sure can and before that lets listen to what they would be saying now.

We can do that, Kevin asked.

Of course, in today's technology nothing is impossible. He used the controls that he had and pushed a few buttons and the monitor reads, Bug turned Listener.

Now they were able to hear a lot of keyboard tapping and some voice that says, Marco wake up, wake up.

Marco slowly opened his eyes and he was dehydrated.

How did I get here?

That is not important, what is important is, what information did you share with the people who abducted you? Nothing as I knew nothing. They said they would hurt my family and so I gave them Steve.

Who are those people? I don't know them. I haven't seen them before.

Check these photographs, are they these people.

Nopes, the lady.. I'm not sure, she resembles her, but I'm certain, it was not her. She spoke Portuguese with a very heavy accent and she looked local.

Alright! Now you have to pay for luring Steve into their hideout.

But where is Steve?

I can make some arrangements for you to meet him, do you want to meet him?

He smelled a rat, No; I don't want to meet him.

Leonardo took his gun, aimed at his knee and shot him. You would be crippled for life that is the punishment that I would like to give you for betraying your brother.

He yelled out in pain and at that time, it was the best thing that I could do? No Leonardo, please stop, I won't be able to do anything now, please don't hurt me more. I have a family to take care off.

We are the brothers and sisters of this fraternity; we should be your first family. Well, you lured Steve with your tongue. Leonardo signaled to hold him tight, he used a Weitlaner retractor, mainly used during the surgical procedures to pull out Marco's tongue and using a surgical blade, he cut that in half.

With a pool of blood around him, he said now you won't be able to lure anyone and betray us. Next time, you have that thought, you will think about the leg and the tongue that you have lost and you won't feel like betraying us again.

In case your leg is alright, come back to me and I can give you another job in this fraternity, to feed my pets. Now get out of here.

With lots of pain, Marco crawled and his people took him by his hands and threw him into a car, which dropped him outside his house.

Meanwhile, the three amigos who were listening to conversation got shell shocked because of the way Leonardo treated his people.

And they were getting ready for phase II of their investigation with the data that they have collected so far from multiple sources. Need a few more answers to straighten this out.

Kevin and Ambra were talking to each other over a glass of wine, Brandon was busy on his computer, trying to connect the dots and getting all information that they would require to take the next step.

31

Ambra, Brandon called, going forward you need to keep in mind about the inevitable. We know that your father has not called and have disappeared in Turkey. And I believe that he might have ended up in the hands of Leonardo. Always keep that in mind.

We know the map that has been stored in your fathers personal computer actually belonged to Leonardo and from the look of it, it's old, which means, this could have been passed down the generations like a family legacy or he recently found it from someone. Either-way, he is cruel and at the same time witty, we need to make sure that we run at least two steps in front of him, but with that being said he will soon catch up with us and that is inevitable.

I just asked a question to check whether he knows anything about us...

Before he could complete, Ambra said about him being at the airport.

You are smart, Ambra, said Kevin.

Yes! The question about him being at the airport; which means he knows who we are and what we are looking, but we have an upper edge, he doesn't know that your father has deciphered the contents in that paper that he lost. But as a matter of fact, now all he knows is that we are trying to find your father and he is worried that the case would open up possibilities to put him behind bars and if he has seen my face in the military database, he wouldn't keep quiet until he finds more about me and about the missions that I have commanded. He will see that soon, before that we necessitate to understand and check the path that your father walked.

In-order for us to take the next step, we need to decipher the map to understand why he was in Turkey. Kevin interrupted, you said you have the map. Yes! He had saved it on his home computer and I have a copy of that in my computer now. Time to get a print out and infer the map and start joining the points. We need to do that soon.

My father took close to a year before he could decipher it. I know for sure that he has run it against many tools that he has and still he had to depend on his skills to decipher it.

It's definitely worth a try and we need to commemorate that time is of the essence. We do not have the luxury of time that your father had. Leonardo hunted for him, but he was not able to get close to him because he stayed low and we didn't. And by the looks of it, he might have started his search for us in and around this hotel as we lured both into the basement of this hotel. They don't know the place, but they know the locality where they were captured from and he might start his search in this area first. And I would be doing the exact same thing if I was in his position.

As they spoke, Brandon opened his computer, took a print out of the map. And gave a copy to everyone the minute that we decipher, destroy all the other copies and we will just keep the one that we deciphered. We cannot take any chances and we need to make sure that we are going go out as a team and from now on no way, that one of us would roam around. Even if we have to, we would carry our phones with us and that will help us track where each of us are; especially you Ambra, please do not get out unaccompanied. Currently we are under a lot of scrutiny and we cannot take any chances. Hope you got me.

Kevin said we would require a larger team to track the team who is tracking us. Do you have anybody in mind Brandon?

Brandon smiled and looked at Kevin.

No, you are not serious are you? Do you have a better plan?

Kevin, the best of the best – we don't really know where they are and we just need them to work for us from where they are.

Absolutely, track them.

Who are you talking about? Our Team, our elite team of Eagle I.

Brandon took his cell phone and punched in "Code Red" and send it a list that he stored on his phone, even Kevin received that message.

Kevin looked at Brandon; you need to be online for this, while Ambra and Kevin were busy looking at the paper that Brandon gave trying to decipher the code. Brandon was busy replying to the email explaining the statistics that he wanted from his group.

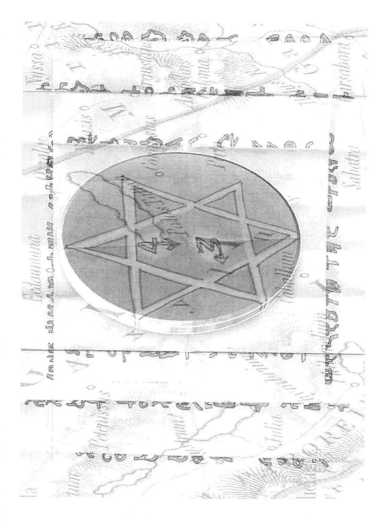

32

Eagle I – the most trusted name in the force. They are the chosen ones for all high profile cases. They have had missions in the most dangerous parts of the world.

From rescue missions to destroying the whole place, they have made their presence felt. They were mean and knew how to get an answer that they require in the most painful way. That is because they were paid to do that. Their identities were always kept in the confirmed dead database of the armed forces. They were successful in each and every mission that they took over.

There were people for every aspect of the case, there were GPS experts, DNA Profiler, Language expert, computer expert – an expert to hack into any system within a matter of minutes and get the details on to their system, sharp shooters, torture specialist, map readers, everything that they wanted to have the mission successful. And the best part was that, this was confined to a 5 member team. Both Brandon and Kevin had the privilege to work among those elites.

They were always together for any mission and if any help was required, they were always there to protect each other and see to that each one them received the help that they wanted at any given point of time.

One of their missions was to get back the daughter of a very highly reputed individual, which was almost like an impossible task. She was kept in a basement of an abandoned house somewhere in Scotland and that was the only thing that we knew. They have thirty six hours before the ransom is paid to get her released and her parents were ready to pay the ransom.

The mission was not to talk to her parents, but rescue her unharmed. Identifying the location was the primary task, this is where the GPS expert and a computer expert came into their play, they tapped into her parents' phone line and a computer, accessed her father's finances to check the latest in flow on money and they were able to find out there was a huge amount of money that was credited into her father's account couple of weeks back as a payment for a huge shipment.

They knew, it had to be someone who knew about this transfer, so their primary task was to identify who all knew about this money coming in, in-order for that,

Mr. Torture went into the finance managers' house to understand who all knew about this shipment and who all were involved in crediting this amount into the bank. With wasting much time, the manager provided all the information that they required.

Their second task was to run those names against the entire name in the database of known criminals and their known associates. Out of which five names had a hit two from England and three from the States; next phase was to understand if there is a link between all of them. And they have all served the same prison at the same time in the same block, coincidence at its peak.

They took the nearest person into custody for interrogation and again, Mr. Torture was sent to question him.

He went in and said before I ask you something, let me make this very clear, every wrong answer or if I feel the answer is wrong, you would pay for it with your body, so it is your duty to put the icing on the cake and give me the exact words that I wanted to hear.

He just smiled and Mr. Torture reciprocated.

Where is she? Who are you talking about?

He took a surgical blade from his kit and made a wound on his hand.

Is this the best that you can do? He smiled and took a garden scissors and cut his tiny finger off.

She is Scotland, Aberdeen to be exact.

Fantastic! Where in Aberdeen? I don't know, all I have is a few numbers and this is what they have shared with us. They said the lesser we know the better.

What numbers are talking about? 5724878-206749

What are these numbers? I don't know, I swear I don't know.

Alright! Imagine I understand what these numbers are, where I can find them, there would be an abandoned house and look for a yellow cloth outside that house. That's all I know, I swear. The girl is there.

So what are you planning to do with the girl once the ransom is paid, they would kill her to ensure that there are no witnesses and nobody is coming back for them.

We thought as much. And thank you for your co-operation.

Take me to a doctor please. I beg of you. Doctor?

You kidnapped someone who is just 9 years old; imagine her mental trauma that she is currently going through. I'm going to leave you here for some time with these rats for your company; if you are alive when I get back, then I will think about taking you to a doctor. Wouldn't that be nice? Until then, Adios Amigo.

He got out and started looking at those numbers, any idea, what those numbers are? Nopes.

I wouldn't say that, they all turned around and it was Mr. Map is standing there. What do you mean? You asked where in Aberdeen and he gave you those numbers. And I matched it to a location on the map, that was the latitude and longitude that he provided, it is a place called Balmedie. Sea route would be the easiest to get there and would have to drive a little, but our big task now is to locate the house. Let us worry about it, said Mr. GPS.

He triangulated all the signals in and around the house of that elite individual, whose name shall not be said; also triangulated all the communication signals coming from Balmedie.

Within no time, due to their luck, they called, they called to check whether the money is ready and to let them know to anticipate their call one hour prior to their drop time for the drop location.

Yes! We got them. Now it's time for action. Let's gear up boys and let's have our bird in the air as this is going to be one heck of an operation. Team, keep in mind, all we know is that there are two people from England involved in this, but we are unsure of how many people are going to be there in that house, protecting their investment. Our only aim is to get the girl unharmed and make sure that she is in safe hands.

Rest, let the police take care, in terms of getting the answers for whom, why and when?

Our mission ends when the girl is safe. The code for this operation is "Freedom"

They were all geared up and they were dropped into the sea near Balmedie and they swam across to get to the shore. The time was around 4:00AM, they dropped their bags, changed their wet clothes, and loaded all the arms and ammunitions and they all went on separate ways to address using the tracker.

The house was initially covered and just as that man said there was a yellow cloth outside the house flying in the air.

The house was heavily guarded and without wasting much time, the Eagle I started their attack taken them one by one, without making a sound, they entered the house and gave hand signals about the number of people on each side and they took them as well.

They opened all the doors in-order to find the door that leads to the basement, they were not able to track that door, immediately, some gadgets came out of the pocket of Mr. Computer and without much time, he had the plan of the house on his system and the path to the basement was through a door that is there on the floor, hidden under the bed.

When the girl was found, they used their radio to inform their leaders about the finding, the words said "Mission Freedom Successful with 22 confirmed dead"

The joy of her parents knew no bounds as they hugged their daughter again.

The mission was successful in 22 hours.

Now that's us, that's EAGLE I for you, Ambra. Brandon said.

33

Hello, Room Service. How may I help you?

I would order a bottle of scotch, chicken wings and the chefs special for today. Do you guys want something? Brandon asked.

No we are good for the time being said Ambra. Speak for yourself lady, make the food items for two and we will share the scotch if it's ok with you? I'm good.

Ambra said I will take a black coffee though, not sure how long I would have to be awake trying to decipher this.

And a black coffee, please.

Sure Sir, will send it to your room in less than 30 minutes.

Thank you, said Brandon.

They sat on the bed and shared some jokes and had a hearty laugh and while they were doing this, they heard a knock on the door and a shout – Room Service.

Brandon opened the door, signed the receipt and said I will take it from here. Thank you.

He took the tray in and closed the door behind him and opened the bottle of Glenfiddich, poured half a glass, raised the glass as a toast and emptied it one sip. Nobody is a guest here so please help yourself.

Kevin had some whiskey as well, while Ambra poured her coffee. The conversation and laughs that they had ended abruptly, having had their share they diverted the attention to the printout that Brandon provided trying to understand the contents.

Why can't they have a piece of paper that says dig here and you will find the treasure rather than giving us a roundabout? They ignored Ambra's comments.

Kevin took his computer loaded the image to his computer and started running the decipher tool and hoping a hit, but in the mean all the three minds were restless, they were trying all the possible permutations and combinations.

Soon the bottle of Whiskey was history, the food on the table were more than half eaten. Sleep was in their eyes, Ambra was not able to resist it and she was fast asleep without any time. Kevin after moving away from the force, he was proper days and nights and he also was not able to resist his sleep for a long time.

Brandon on the other hand has been practicing what he learnt to think that what if another situation in life appears and he is currently facing one.

Brandon was awake, he took a Rubik cube in his hand was busy thinking how he can crack it. Was mentally doing all the calculations trying to decipher it and he wanted to crack this case wide open and the most pivotal evidence is there in right front of him and he is not able to sleep, keeping that in mind.

He was writing something, throwing the paper away and nothing was working out. After some time, he got bored and he started creating paper planes and was trying to fly it, like being a young boy who was fascinated by his little toys. And it suddenly struck him.

He went back to his computer, looked at the image again and this time, he had a clue how to crack it, now all he wants is a couple more clues to make sure that he is reading it the right way.

He sat on a chair with his legs resting on the table, head up and closed his eyes, he was going through the image on his head over and over. He sat down and was not getting any rest until he is able to understand the image or decipher the map completely.

He looked at his watch, time was 5:00AM and he knew that one of them is going to wake up now and before that he wanted to finish the map before that.

He looked at the software that Kevin was running; it was over, the monitor said 'Not in an understandable format'.

He slowly took a pencil and took the printout, and he slowly numbered certain things and he let go a sign of relief.

It was, Ambra who woke up first and from the look of the room, she understood that Brandon would have just slept; Brandon was sitting on the chair with his legs rested on the table and was fast asleep. She looked at Kevin and she knew that he went to bed almost at the same time she fell asleep.

She didn't bother to wake them up and she washed her face and changing her clothes to go out for a coffee, she remembered, Brandon says that whatever happens we won't leave the sight of each other. So she took the phone and ordered a coffee for her through Room Service.

In ten minutes, there was a knock on the door, she peeped to make sure that it was room service, just like Brandon did, she said I will take it up from here and tipped the waiter.

Made a coffee and had it by the window, she could see a lot papers everywhere, including the toy planes, she smiled and she searched for Brandon's print out as she was lazy to walk to the bed lean and take her print out. But she was not able to find his print out. So she didn't have another and she was looking at the paper in all directions, including turning it around and trying to read the contents from the corner of the paper.

She finished her coffee and she was keeping the cup on the table nearby, she could see that Kevin is turning around and the gun that he was hiding fell out and in that sound both Kevin and Brandon woke up. But Brandon was too tired to listen or to hear the explanation of what happened, he walked over to the bed and fell on it; Kevin could understand the tiredness and he was definitely not getting younger.

Brandon woke up after a while and they were still hanging onto the paper that they had, any luck? He asked in a sleepy tone.

Yeah! Kevin said and Ambra looked in surprise? What is it? Brandon inquired. I'm hungry and this is a double bonded paper.

Brandon woke up and went to the wash room, brushed his teeth and washed his face and came out.

I broke the code. I know what it means now. And Brandon stood there with pride.

Well, what were you waiting for?

Christmas I guess.

While you morons slept, I stayed awake trying to break the code doing my permutations and combinations and now when I wanted to sleep you are saying that you are not ready to wait and try to decipher the contents and you are telling me that I should have told you before I closed my eyes.

Brandon, time is of essence you told me that, Well Ambra it's like this, time is not in our hands, can we outsmart time, I think not. But you guys slept peacefully throughout the night. Everybody needs rest, time or no time, I want to rest as well.

And as a matter of fact, I wanted to see how smart you were. Just wanted to check if you were able to crack it, anyways it's an easy one. And let me tell you how I have cracked it, now this is my logic, probability of this is going to be correct ninety percent.

They smiled as Brandon started to explain.

34

Leonardo was sitting in a corner of his huge room trying to plan his next moves. He didn't have a starting point as he knew he was dealing with a professional. He was looking for a lead to start with. It never crossed his mind that they are after the contents of the paper, as Ambra been accompanied, he was sure that they are trying to find her father.

He was trying to find out their hideout. He has already given instructions to his partners in crime to flash around their photographs in all the types of high and low places; he thought that would give him a lead to start with, in terms of understanding where they stay. But that was a dead end, after days of searching in each and every hotel in town, none of them recognized them.

He had a team hacking into every surveillance camera in the town and running it against the facial recognition software and whatever it is once the camera picks it up, he would get a trace where they go, but that again was a dead end, their faces were never captured by any of the cameras so far.

He knew, he cannot be frustrated, the more impatient he became less the chances are to find them, as he wouldn't be thinking with the right frame of mind. So every now and then, he feels angry, he fills his lungs with lots of air by taking deep breaths and telling him softly relax, calm down until the anger passes away, but he had to do that more often than he thought he might and more than thinking he was taking deep breaths.

Leonardo is a cautious fighter. He was not ready to give up easily, even though he knew that sooner or later they would fall into his hands. The leader inside him didn't want that, he wanted to lead; he wanted to know every single step that they took and he wanted them in his clutches before they come to him.

He has managed to stay ahead of every department in the world, understanding their every move and staying updated and making sure that he stays out of their sight.

Out of their sight; to catch a crook you need to think like a crook and to catch a cop you need to think like one. They know to stay away from me, they either need to hide in a place that I wouldn't look or they would be hiding in plain sight. And there is also a possibility that they are getting a helping hand here. What if they have a portable set of all the equipments that is required for them to keep me in surveillance or they have the equipments to make sure that the things are falling in place. Cops, they ought to have helped wherever they go by hook or by crook, they would find like minded people somewhere to give them a helping hand.

Who? Is there someone like that. He had techies who would help him barge into any calls that is happening across the globe, which actually helped him to stay out of prison for a long time and the names like Leo, Leonardo, Carunio… certain words that would trigger the reaction and his people could listen into those calls to check if there are any possible threats against him and he would get his warning instantly, so this time.

He took his cell phone and asked the techies to add certain more key words like Ambra, Brandon, Franco and I wanted to know if anything clicks and possibly, we might get a hit and we would get a starting point or even better, we would be able to know their whereabouts.

There reached a time where he was not able to manage the anger. He could smell the air that is filled with smoke. Smoke from a corpse burning into ashes. He could feel the shiver in his body. He was not able to concentrate when the air is fresh and he had to create a scene in which he is comfortable with. He was taking a mental trip to his happy place. Worse than a cemetery, bodies getting burned, people eating the burned flesh that gets on a projectile as the corpse burned to ashes. He could smell it and could feel it. He stood there in the middle of that place, a place that would be a nightmare for others; the leeches started to crawl up his body to drink the blood, people waiting there to pounce on him for raw flesh and they looked at him as they saw the juiciest flesh. He stood there in silence. He could feel like a million volt of electricity been passed through his body, he could feel the pain, his teeth rattled; he was building the mood that is required to get back on track. To make it even more real, he reached for the twin vase from a nearby table with his eyes closed and broke it into a million pieces by hitting it on his head The blood started to ooze out and he was in pain, he punched the wall multiple times until his hands bled and he continued the action. And he was able to control his emotions better. With the smell of the burnt corpse, people waiting to pounce on him alive, leeches on his body, as he stood there in that open space where he was happy with the pain, he was able to release his anger and made him think straight. A way to get better of them rather sitting on this piece of shit and waiting for things to happen.

What is that I can do, to get them into my clutches? Need to lead, to get to them.

Steve's phone that got tossed under the table may be that would give me a place to start.

35

Brandon got out of the bed and took the map in his hand and as he was about to explain how to read the map and the message that was deciphered.

His phone rang, it says – Unknown Number.

He got confused.

He answered the phone; Hi.

You don't want to know who I'm but the enemy of my enemy is my friend.

This is a secured line. How did you get this number?

That is the least of your worries, if I can find you and if I can trace you, so can Leonardo. I don't have much time, probably by now, this call would be tracked and the signals would be triangulated.

I wouldn't worry about that.

Neither would I

What is that you want?

As I said the enemy of my enemy is my friend and I would be able to give you a helping hand in every step you take and would even give you tips how to save your ass.

I'm listening

In the meantime, Brandon signaled Kevin to track that call and to understand the whereabouts. Kevin rushed to his computer and the search was on and also has sent messages to Mr. Computer to track his phone and try to locate who he is speaking to. They were on to it.

Listen and listen carefully.

The minute Leonardo gets to you, you can kiss your good ass good bye. But with me in the picture you would be able to save it. And for me to be in that picture, you need to trust me completely. You may not know who I'm and what I'm planning and you shouldn't try to poke at and try to find my whereabouts. If that's a deal that you can comply, I can assure your success in finding the truth about Ambra's father. And who killed him and why?

Kevin was listening into the call, they looked at each other and they looked at Ambra; she didn't understand that look and they kept it that way.

Gotcha, now what?

He would have started his hunt for you and he would tear you apart if you were in his hands.

You are saying that because you don't know me well.

What is there is to know? Being on the military's elite team and have commanded a hundred or more missions in place that a few of us are not privileged to know, master of weapons and master of martial arts, but what good is all that in front of a loaded gun, hands tied to the back. Until and unless you are Houdini to get out of that and can make a hundred loaded guns aiming at you from different locations, probably including snipers from different building disappear and leave them confused as you vanish into a smoke like a ninja. Would you be able to do that?

Brandon was appalled. He couldn't believe his ears. Someone knew his past and questioning his expertise. He didn't know what to do and he was overwhelmed with emotions.

After a moment of silence, he spoke again. I trust you. What is that I need to do? And where did you find my details.

Let's just say, I have my sources. Just note, Leonardo would be hearing this conversation with the state of the art equipments that he has. So just be careful, but my phone and your phone are secured and finding where we are speaking from would be out of the question.

I can read your mind, maybe not now, but soon enough. You will know who I'm and my intentions a little later.

You still didn't answer my question, what is that I need to do now?

Stay out of trouble; currently do not get keen with Leonardo. You will get him sometime soon, until then have patience and that is not the reason why you are here, never deviate from the plan, focus on what you are here for and I will make sure that I will guide you in each step of the way and I would be able to provide you with invaluable information which is going to help you as we all move forward.

All you need to know now is that, I have my agenda and you have yours, but both these agenda's will coincide with each other as you move forward, until then, allow me to help you.

Currently, just focus on your plan; don't deviate.

As of now, you trust me and I trust you. So this conversation needs to be both ways. As we speak, there is an application that is getting installed on your phone. Do not worry, that is not for me to track you, it is for you to contact me. All you have to do is dial seven on your phone and it would connect to me. And in case I'm busy, be assured that I would call you back.

Thank you.

No, I should be thanking you because you are going to be a big help for me to complete my plan of action.

Will talk again and the line went dead.

36

Leonardo on the other end was listening on to the call. Who is this Brandon? And how did he get his number, I was not able to get so much detail about him, but on the other end he was about to get his details. How is that possible?

Sir…

Give me some good news now, where you able to locate his position?

Unfortunately, both of them were using secured phone and the signals were jumping every 15 seconds.

Alright! Give me the starting tower and all the subsequent towers, maybe we will be able to narrow it down.

I'm not sure, Sir, if that is possible. The call came from Australia and it was jumping signals from Australia, to New Zealand to Thailand to India, it was skipping countries and not to mention, it has never touched any of the same towers twice.

What about the receiving end?

Same case, it was also jumping signals from country to country.

If that is the case, my dear.. Why the hell did you call me for?

Sir! One voice that you have heard is of Brandon. And the other voice is of someone who is careful enough to change his voice through a voice modulator software.

What do you mean by that?

We have lots of voice modulation applications that are available in the market and if you actually search over the internet, you may even get some free, but that is the not the point here. The point here is, the other person, if he has to use voice modulation software, there is a probability that either he knows you or he knows Brandon directly. But again, thinking about the possibilities, on a hunch, I would say that this may even be a call to throw us out off track and to confuse us even further.

All three are possible. Very good hunch, but now we need to pick one from the list or we need to go with all three. What would you do suggest that we do?

To start with, I would say, all of us who are using a phone that is connected to a secured server need to be verified, to check how the signal travels and we will narrow it down and we will make sure that it is not one of us who is dealing with it and then we will focus on the third possibility of getting a confirmation whether that was a confusing call or a call that we can hold on to. As this is the first of its kind and if no such calls in the future appears; the reason why I believe that this is a crank call is that, no information was provided over the phone all he said was to stay away from and stay focused on the issue at hand but at the same time information about Brandon was disclosed, what if he wanted to us know what we are dealing with here and he just wanted to perk our curiosity to a level where we get slightly nervous before we could react or come up with a plan. If that is false, then we will move towards the second possibility whether we have someone in our clan that doesn't belong to us. Why I took this as the last resort is because, we don't want to alarm anyone who is currently associated with us, but now the possible question that you currently have would be, wouldn't that person be alarmed when we start checking our phones on the security level of signals. Not really, sir, because only a very hand few people has that kind of secured phone and all of them are trustworthy and they wouldn't disclose this information to anyone else in our fraternity.

Very good thought and you take the lead in this and carry with all the action that might be necessary to nail this down and moreover, if found, I don't want to see their face again, and they would have to bite the bullet no matter what.

That would definitely be a first step. Secondly, I want this phone to be stripped and search this phone and we need to very careful in doing that, from call history to text message, software to hardware, I want to know everything about this phone and everyone on the contact list. This is Steve's phone and make it one hundred percent sure that this phone is searched thoroughly.

We now have two steps to start in two different directions and let's walk together in two different paths.

But actually sir, I would say, we currently have three different paths to travel.

Which one did I miss?

As per the conversation that we heard, he talked about Brandon and what he did when he was in the military and I'm certain that we would be able to get some information about the cases that he worked. And his full name is Brandon Brookes, we should be able to narrow this down about him and his known associates from the files that may be archived in the military database and let start rolling.

Fantastic! You are making this look good. Let's make sure that we travel in all the three paths to understand where will all this lead to.

I'm just worried about the fact or the situation that I may have to face, when he actually finds out about the demise of Franco Gallo and I'm sure that the investigation would knock on my door, thinking I may have been involved in this and I don't want to give them any reason why they need to follow me on this.

And I want to stop that from happening. Not because I don't have time or courage to face that, it is just the impatient times that you need to sit in the court for the umpteenth time and walk away without being charged and pay my lawyer's for this.

We all need to be careful and in the mean time, keep Brandon in check and let us be ready to start travelling in the paths that we have finalized.

37

Leonardo has the state of the art equipments and technology at his fingertips. And a lot of people who may not have a college degree, but excellent in what they do. Would he do such a stupid thing to trace my number and give me a warning?

Don't be childish Brandon, studying our subject, I came to know something, he won't give you any warnings, he would just finish you off and more importantly, if he knew who you were and if he has your secured phone number, he would be knocking on our door by now.

Knock Knock!

There you go; speak of the devil, said Ambra. Who is this?

Room Service! They all left a sign of relief at that time.

Ambra opened the door and said Thank you! I have been waiting for breakfast.

What was that phone call all about?

I don't know, all I could make out from that call is that is that, it is a voice modulated call and some keystrokes here and there. But felt like I could trust him.

Kevin said even I think we could trust him.

Can I listen to that call now?

Brandon was standing in the corner room, watching the view outside near the window, he turned towards Kevin and looked at him and nodded as if he signed to say no. He walked towards Ambra and he said we do not have much time here. We need to make sure that we do not leave any evidence in this hotel and leave this place by night. Kevin is now making sure that we would get our transportation out of here and we are going to get out of this place alive using the very same method that we used to come in. The only difference this time is we are not going to use the private jet, the reason being, he might have kept a note on that flight charter planning as he knew, this aircraft has been here for quite some time and he might think that he would get a lead, when that airplane takes off. Hence we are going to buy our tickets on a different airline and would need to move out of this place by morning.

What about the phone call, can I listen?

Of course you can, said Brandon, but before that, we need to make sure that our flight tickets and lodging are taken care of in Turkey.

Yes! Turkey, did you get any clue why my father went to Turkey.

As a matter of fact, I do know why your father went to Turkey, pay attention and its all because of the contents in this piece of paper.

You are right, you were about to tell us about the code that was inscribed on that paper. What does it say and how did you crack it. This took my dad close to a year to break it and none of the applications that he owned was able to give him a helping hand in deciphering this thing.

How did you do it?

I did it and that is what is important right now. And now, are you closer to understanding why your dad chose me to giving you a helping hand rather than anyone else.

I can see the reason why? Now before both of us hear how you broke the code and the contents of in that paper, let me listen to that phone call.

Brandon, I know you will shout at me when I say this, I forgot to record the call in the midst when I am trying to trace the location.

Damn Kevin.

I know, I'm to blame for this, out of service and out of touch of all the actions. I need to get my basics back together.

Brandon walked towards Kevin, patted on his shoulders and whispered, Good Job. Thank you! We don't want Ambra to listen to this call. Please try sending that call to the Mr. Computer expert and if he can make any head or tail about this call and give us a lead to find this person. And with all probability I feel, that person is going to be our short cut to Leonardo.

Ambra frustrated, there I go, out of luck again. Anyways, now let's hear the content in that letter that lured my dad to Turkey and made him vanish into thin air. I doubt; I seriously doubt that my father is not alive. I think he has kicked the bucket. I feel it and I know it, as we are dealing with a mad son a gun here, who does anything to make sure he gets what he wants and doesn't see the tear in the eyes of the loved ones who are on the losing end. He will pay for what he did and we will make him pay for what he did. If I'm getting an opportunity to finish him, I will be like a wave that takes the life of the one that previously shored, but remember, the wave is pulling back the silent ones to make sure that it rises tall and strong, like I'm going to. I will rise, above and beyond their imagination and if they are responsible in any way, be assured that I'm doing it for all the those who have lost their fathers, mothers, wife, sons and daughters and to the entire mankind, wiping away a mad person from this weird world and with his death, if any tear falls on this face of earth, that there won't harm in any way, but instead it would spread the warmth of love that it was shed in the first place. Nothing more, Nothing less.

38

Leonardo, I have got news for you. Good you may presume, but I'm not sure how you are going to take it. I tried our entire secured phone and tried to analyze their signals without anyone of them knowing it and that at multiple times just to be sure and see if there is a pattern. Well, as a matter of fact, all our secured networks were jumping from tower to tower within this small place and have never left the country. So we can rule out if any one of our people is using that kind of service.

I couldn't move into our third possibility of checking whether the call was just to throw us off, as that person never contacted Brandon yet. And moreover, we need to make sure that things are falling in place, so I moved into our second possibility of checking our associates, just to double check and I went back into their files and all the new recruits in the last 4 years, were brought by our most trusted people that we work with and none of them were flagged and more importantly, I double checked all the resources in all the databases and have found at least one or two cases associated with them from armed robbery to smuggling. But none of them were associated with this call so far.

With that being said this is the most interesting part that I wanted you to hear and please give me your complete attention on this. I stripped this phone as you have asked me to; I found this bug in this phone. This is just not a chip; this is the next level of intelligence. Fantastic discovery, this chip cannot be replicated and has to be made in a very closed environment, the best algorithm that I have seen as this is hack proof, water proof and doesn't come with a circuit. So, I had to virtually breakdown this chip, in the virtual environment, this chip got self destroyed and was unable to track it, but fortunately, the virtual imaging was complete and we have a picture of this chip now. As I said this cannot be replicated, completely hack-free.

Now the beauty of this chip is that, this has a two way communication system when the person is talking on the phone, which means, the person who bugged this phone, could not only hear and record the conversation, but can talk to both the parties, if need be; not only that, that person could get the phone number of all the parties attending the call, however, secured the line is. Most importantly, when the phone is not functioning, as in if the phone is on and if the person is not talking, this chip will act as a listening device to at least twenty five square radius; that is something new. Not only that, this chip will record the conversation of all the phones in its range and will release a virus through the network and can get the information of all the contacts, calendars, anything and everything that is stored on the phones, tablets, computers that is in the range of that chip, which means, by now Brandon has all the required information by now. All our phone numbers, contacts from each number, calendar entries, everything from our phones; I'm not talking about one or two of them, from everyone who were present in this house at that time and not only that, this phone was lying under the table for long enough for Brandon to collect all the details.

Now the interesting part, I can serial number on that chip against the hardware, databases that have, this is a new invention and this serial number is registered to the armed forces central command center. No names and no numbers.

Finally, as I know you would be interested to know more about Brandon, I tried hacking into the secondary server as now I got a name "Central Command Center" I got into their database and I could get more information about Brandon Brookes.

Brandon Brookes – still active in the force, but not to many, he has been leading a retired life for a long time as he and his group would participate only in the elite and high profile cases that requires immediate attention. During other times the entire group leads a very normal life like other people and nobody knows who they are or where they are from and where they are currently. They all have their secured phone in motion which would allow the command center to contact them when need be. I tried to locate Brandon Brookes in any of the surveillance cameras across the United States, but this man is very careful not to give his face to any camera and of course, they are trained machines to understand a threat is on its way. Known associates – couldn't get any, but I'm sure there are many and they all hide under our plain sight, which makes it even harder to capture them. He is trained in martial arts; got a Masters in Paleontology, Sharp shooter as he knows each and every weapon known to man, its make and how precisely it would be in close and far range. This man is a walking weapon by himself.

Leonardo listened to all this very carefully and asked where this secondary server is or this central command center located?

Well, what is the most interesting part, the command center is located in Groom Lake a few miles away from the most happening cities in the world, Las Vegas, this place is commonly known as Area 51. The server was not easy to hack.

Do we have a face for the actual Brandon and not just the ones that we saw?

Yes! We do, he did some typing on his tablet and the phone is there on your phone …. Now.

Leonardo opened his phone and saw the face. It was the same one whom he saw in all the time. But this one was different, Sharp blue eyes, salt and pepper hair do and well combed, the only difference from then and now is that now Brandon has a French beard.

What next inquired his associate?

Track him, now that you told me that he knows all the phone numbers, he would definitely have mine and mine would be on his watch list to record or for even live listening. This means he has given me a window of opportunity to lure him here.

All I have to do now is make a phone call, which would sound as a threat to him and get him to place where we could watch me do the business and make him walk right into my trap.

Yes! That is a possibility and worth a shot.

39

Ambra, getting angry is not going to get you anywhere, with that being said anger is good, it would not allow you to have peace with your enemy especially in a situation like this. The fight is not good, it hurts people, that's we also try to avoid fights in all possible scenarios, but if you must fight.. WIN.

Being intelligent is not the sign of being wise, but if you think again, neither is common sense. There is a fine line between wisdom and common sense. Common sense lets you keep your mouth shut when need be, but on the other hand wisdom would tell you which weapon to use at the right time. There is no point taking a knife to a gun fight and similarly, there is no point in taking a rocket launcher to kill someone at point blank. What I'm trying to tell you is that, you will get your chance, a face to face rendezvous with Leonardo and that point of time, don't think of your brain; think using your heart. That is the fine line between common sense and wisdom.

I understand Brandon; it's the pain that he has put me through all this. Now that the past, let's focus on the present and tell me what made my dad be on that flight all the way to Turkey.

And I thought you might have forgotten all about it. Do you actually give up and not wanting to wait a little more and try a little harder, so that I can close my eyes for some minutes before you give up again. You know what, why don't you tell me what it is and I will let you sleep, until we make the arrangements to get on a plane that would take us out of here.

That is a good idea, Kevin interfered.

In that case, you both of sit here and let me explain this to you, how I cracked it. Now on this map, do you see a number on each of these markings; that is the order how it needs to be read. Secondly, you see the numbers are repeated in certain markings, for example, you see a one here on top of this and one beneath this on the opposite side. Now if I fold this paper and join this together, it will show you the complete alphabet. Now these are ancient Hebrew alphabets.

How did you decipher that it was an ancient Hebrew alphabet? Ambra questioned.

Ah! That was the beauty, once I understood the alphabet, I scanned the letter again and took one alphabet from this and ran it against the available resources like the web pages, databases, all over the internet and that gave me a hit; which made me realize that it is written in a script that belonged to the ancient Hebrews. This thing here, which looks like a seven, if you turn the paper, is 'L'; then I took one by one and translated this to English, which of course was not an easy task. I was able to break all of them, apart from this star in the middle and the numbers corresponding to it, but I guess, we have a starting point now and I assume that we will understand what this means as this journey progresses.

Ambra was impressed. What does this mean? Can you tell me what we have here so far? I'm very curious to know where is this is going to take us from now, I'm getting shivers in my body just to know that I'm finally going to learn what this means and why my dad disappeared and where is this going to take me.

But before you tell me anything further, let me ask you this, are we going to sit on fire when we come to know the meaning of this and are we going to get pushed into a dangerous situation that it would be hard for us to get out of.

What difference is it going to make? Aren't we in a dangerous zone already? Now let's continue to pursue the track by connecting the dots and see where it is going to lead us next.

Going by the numbers, it means

1. Look for Rose
2. Beneath the stars
3. The Thickest Tree
4. Pull in Phrygia

And then you have this star in the center with corresponding number in two legs of the star three and four, which I haven't deciphered yet. But if you see, the fourth clue, it says, "Pull in Phrygia" – If I have deciphered this correctly, this is what took your father all the way to Turkey.

In antiquity, Phrygia was a kingdom in the west central part of Anatolia, in what is now Turkey, centered around the Sakarya River. Phrygian power reached its peak in the late 8th century BC under another, historical king Midas, who dominated most of western and central Anatolia and rivaled Assyria and Urartu for power in eastern Anatolia. This later Midas was, however, also the last independent king of Phrygia before its capital Gordium was sacked by Cimmerians around 695 BC. Phrygia then became subject to Lydia, and then successively to Persia, Alexander and his Hellenistic successors, Pergamon, Rome and Byzantium. The Phrygians were gradually assimilated into other cultures by the early medieval era, and after the Turkish conquest of Anatolia the name Phrygia passed out of usage as a territorial designation.

And you know this how? Ambra was interested.

Easy! We have Google and Wikipedia – What are they for, I by hearted this entire thing last night and Brandon looked at Ambra and said just to impress you. Ambra smiled.

Kevin got in between them, now we know what took Franco to Turkey, our initial and the main reason why we are here in Brazil has officially come to an end; with that being said we have also got a bonus by knowing about Leonardo and about his blood sucking hooligans who are going to tail us from now on. This is going to be fun.

40

B randon went to hit the bed.

Where are we on the reservations in Turkey? Ambra asked.

All taken care; now before Brandon is up, let's start packing and be ready, we will leave around 1:00PM and that doesn't give us each time to uninstall all the equipments that we have here and get ready.

Don't worry about the equipments, I'll take care of that and more over we are not going to take our equipments, as soon as we check into our hotel there our new set of equipments would already be installed there. Two things that we just cannot forget are Brandon's laptop and mine. Rest everything would be awaiting our arrival in Turkey.

And this time, we are not taking my private jet, we are going to use a normal aircraft that would take us to our new location because the minute I charter it,

Leonardo's eyes will fall on that and at this point of time, it is too much a risk that we can take. We need to be there and we will play hide and seek with Leonardo there; I'm sure that Brandon would also have plans around this. Let us see what we have in store for us.

In the meantime, you start with your bag and let me worry about mine. Once we finish our packing, we will start with Brandon's, just make sure that you are not touching his bag, and just keep his stuff arranged here. He will do the rest. That's how he likes it. He wanted to do things on his own.

That's fine with me.

They started packing and in the meantime, Kevin called the hotel reception asking them for a cab that would take them to the airport at 4:00PM. And they were looking in all the corners of the room just to make sure that they are not leaving anything behind for others to find.

Brandon woke up after a few hours just to find that all the things are now placed in order and place is all set. His clothes were kept on the bed. He saw all this and he knew the drill, he went straight to the equipments, opened it and deleted all the applications and data that they used so far, post transferring all the contents of an untraceable hard drive and all the systems were wiped clean even to retrieve the lost data would be impossible.

He took his clothes, folded it neatly and kept it inside his bag. And he did one last search in the room, before he took a shower to freshen himself. They were all ready; the makeup was done and was set to leave to the airport.

The phone rang, just to inform them that the cab is waiting to take them to the airport. Kevin left the room first and proceeded downstairs to clear all the outstanding dues that they might have on his credit card.

While he was doing that, their bags were loaded onto the cab.

They were very careful at the airport, just to make sure that the facial recognition software doesn't capture their faces and throw a result of Leonardo.

This is going to be a long flight. Brandon gave a phone to Ambra, this is your phone. This is currently on a very tight and highly secured network, which means, you can even use this phone inside the aircraft, under a dungeon, never out of range, with a battery backup of seven days without charging. Got a panic button and you can use it anytime and it will start emitting the signal telling us your exact location. Even though you have that, we are not permitted you to go beyond a point alone where our eyes can't catch.

This is going to be fun and adventurous; every single step needs to be taken with caution. One bad choice, probably that would be the last daylight we would see. We are going to be a backup for each other, you guard my back and I guard yours. From this point on, we are going to be inside a wall that we make and those walls are going to be guarded with our trust, brains, guns and courage. We have only those. We are going to be three against a hundred, the minute you understand that you are going to get captured, remember, do not panic, hit the panic button and leave your faith with us and that's how it is for all of us. Keep this ingrained in your head and mind. That "We all will go home"

You are going to face a lot of things on this trip sometimes including torture. Don't give up and don't give in. Read as much as about Turkey on this flight and that information would be useful. We need it. We are three and there are a few who is going to guide us from across the oceans, but that also is not going to guarantee our safety. Our safety comes when we leave our blind faith and trust with each other. You are going to leave your life in my hands, like I trust mine with you. From this moment on, there is no turning back. We cannot afford a wrong move.

Ambra looked outside the window, through the passing clouds, she was nervous, scared and was not able to believe the kind of situation that she was in. All she could see outside in each and every cloud was that – "We all go home".

41

S ir! The facial recognition software identified them with a rent a car service in Turkey.

Are you telling me that, they left Brazil without our knowledge?

As a matter of fact, yes sir! They are currently in Turkey. This Brandon guy was checking out for a car, right in front of a surveillance camera in that store and our equipments captured that.

Leonardo watched the video multiple times in which Brandon is checking out the car, right in front of the security camera. He smiled and said he is trying to lure me to him, when I'm trying to do the exact opposite. There is a trap in this video and you couldn't find that out. None of the computer algorithms would replace a human instinct. You can ask a robot to talk, walk and do whatever we humans do. But do you know the difference between a man and a machine, we can think and we have emotions and most of all it is because, we have instincts. And my instincts are telling me that, this is a trap. This guy has been so very careful while he was here in Brazil and suddenly in Turkey, he comes into our grid, isn't it something that we need to fathom about?

Now that we know where he is, it's time for us to make our entry. Get me a ticket on the next available flight to Turkey, any class would be fine. I want to be there. We need to make sure that get them in one piece, because they would start their hunt for me as soon as they understand that I'm behind all this. I didn't get what I want, but I somehow guess, it is all because of that paper that I lost. Over the generations it has been just a piece of paper that was handed down through generations. And I'm not sure, how it landed up with my family in the first place. But I'm sure, the contents of that piece of paper is something to do with all this. So far, I feel we have been chasing the wrong thing. We have been chasing the paper in terms of where, what and how and trying to retrieve the paper. And in fact, if you think about it, Franco actually gave up his life for that paper, which means, there is something in that paper, that we never chased. And we have been looking at this in a completely different way.

If we were looking at this in a different way, there is a possibility that Ambra and Brandon are not here just to have vengeance against me or to find me, but I guess they are chasing the contents of the letter just like Franco did, which we overlooked. Until and unless we have a copy of that paper or understand the contents, we cannot get to a closure swiftly on this one.

As a first step, let's get to Turkey and understand where they are and what are they up to; from there we will figure out our next move and once we identify where they are, we can go ahead and understand what they are up to.

Leonardo was in the very next flight that was scheduled to Turkey and his men has already arranged for his stay, transport and other nitty-gritties that would required during his stay in Turkey.

As soon as he landed in Turkey, he went straight to the car dealer where Brandon was seen last and took the photograph out of his pocket and asked the person to provide him with the address that he has provided while taking a car for rental.

I'm sorry, sir, but I cannot provide any details of my client, until and unless I see a warrant.

Warrant? Who says we are cops? We are not cops and he took out of a Berretta F and pushed it in his mouth and said you want to give me the details or do you want me to put a nice little hole in your brain. And one of this will happen whether you like it or not, and I guess the hole won't be pleasing to look at. Either way, you won't feel it. If you give it, you will feel happy that you are still breathing; otherwise, we will still take what we want over your dead body.

I will get the information for you. No sweat.

That's a good boy, you learn fast.

He is staying at the Royal Gateways, Room 302.

Thank you and threw some money over to him. And that you slime is for your service and Leonardo and the gang walked out.

As he got into his car, his driver asked him, where we are going now?

Royal Gateways.

42

Room # 302 – Brandon had fixed a bug at the car rental shop for him to make sure that Leonardo has arrived. Brandon was ready, he appeared in front of the camera in that car dealer's outlet for a reason, he wanted to lure Leonardo to Turkey and then take it from there. He was happy that Leonardo is now in town and now the play is on.

Ambra was checking frantically by calling all the places big and small in and around Turkey to locate the place where her father stayed. She was doing that for the past two hours. Brandon went near her, kept his hand on her shoulders to make her turn around and said this is the time that you wanted to hear this. Your father is no more, just as the feeling you got, he has already kicked the bucket. He could see Ambra's eyes filled with tears, but that shouldn't stop us. We now know the reason why he was in Turkey and we also know that we are way ahead of Leonardo, in terms of understanding the content of that paper, but according to him, he was only trying to retrieve what he originally lost and he doesn't know what it is and its worth. We just know it is leading to some place, but we are also in darkness, because we don't know what it is in store for us.

Your father was a great man and I would do anything to help him. Let me ask you this, you won't find the place where your father stayed by calling any of the hotels for a lot of reasons. One: They don't want to reveal that a person was murdered in their hotel; that is reputation loss. Two: they won't tell you about him because they don't know who is calling even if you say, you are his daughter. Three: They are also scared to death about this whole incident and only the hotel management would know something like this has happened, as Leonardo is a very powerful man with money and influence at all the wrong places. You don't want to make a man like him angry. And the reason why he is following; my guess is he was not able to retrieve what he lost. He is still hunting for that and more over; he is also scared understanding about me via that phone call that I received from an unknown number. So we have an upper hand, you need to make peace with the understanding that you have lost your father and you are not even going to get his body to give him your last respect.

But I promise you this, I will make sure that you get Leonardo alive in front of you for that vengeance that is burning deep inside you. This is my promise, as a matter of fact, I've lured Leonardo into Turkey. He has already started his lookout for us. If we panic, there is no way that we can get away from all this, but if we don't, we do have a fighting chance to get cleared and move on. Now we are going to start the second phase of his journey, finding out what is on that map, before we get lured or fall into his trap.

I agree, I completely agree, I wanted to see what my dad saw and what he saw before they put him to sleep. Fighting him and trying to locate the place like in the movies would be a difficult task. The task would be a little easier, if we are not fighting anyone and lead us straight to the treasure or whatever it is. I wanted to see what my dad saw last.

Absolutely! I agree, we can search peacefully when we are not fighting. For that, either we need to make sure that we lure Leonardo into our trap post we get back from that place or we need to make sure that we are also not falling into his trap on the way there.

We would fall into this trap, how? Ambra asked.

Well, your father was here for a long time and I'm certain that your father would have been in his surveillance all throughout from the time he landed in Turkey at the time he was killed. They would have followed him where ever he went, which means, they were behind him even to the closest point wherever this map led. But his men wouldn't be equipped to follow him all the way, otherwise, they would have left us alone and they would have actually waited for us to fall into their trap or would have lured us to theirs. This also means, we would have to take the same road that your father took previously and be sure that Leonardo would be waiting for us in some corner on that road, ready to pounce on us and he won't give up until we kill him or the other way around?

With all this in mind, we are going to take our next step by giving Leonardo a free tip for us and confuse the hell out of him, while we take the road less travelled. And this is the time when our mystery man over the phone is going to help us.

43

Leonardo and his men arrive at the Royal Gateway Hotel, the most luxurious hotel in the city. When they arrived, they were treated by beautiful maidens who were dressed neatly and throwing flowers at them as they entered the hotel. They went to the reception asking for four rooms for them to stay and they wanted it to be as discreet as possible and while filling out the form, they all made sure that they tick the right option, Business or Pleasure, all the them ticked the box, 'Business'. They were handed the key cards and they all proceeded to their respective rooms. Only Leonardo had a separate room for himself, rest every one of them were sharing rooms with each other.

They made sure the corridor was clear for their next step of action. They went to room 302, knocked the door and said Room Service; waited patiently until the door was opened in front of them.

They had a shock again, an old couple opened the room and the lady asked, we didn't order any room service. One of the members said I'm sorry, we might have got the wrong room. By any chance, is Brandon here? Yes, he is taking a shower, he is my husband. Could we meet him, please? Sure! Why not, please come on in and make yourself comfortable.

A couple of them went in and waited again until Brandon made his entry, it was an old man using walker to take every step. It is not every day, I have some visitor. By the way, do we know each other? We are sorry; we thought you were our Boss's school friend Brandon Brookes from United States who served in the military. Oh! I'm sorry to disappoint you; I'm Brandon alright, but not Brandon Brookes. I'm Brandon Messer, never in the military. Yes! We can see that. We are sorry for the inconvenience though. No worries. Now that you are here, can I get you something to drink? No Thank you, we will take our leave now. Sorry again.

They came out of the room and waited till the door was closed in front of them and nodded to Leonardo signing those were not the ones we were looking for.

Leonardo in anger broke a painting on the wall there. But now he knows they are in Turkey and would travel the route that Franco had once travelled. So it is just a matter of time before we get them into our clutches.

They went to the room and Leonardo called his techie back in Brazil to check if they have any update on Brandon or Ambra. They said unfortunately not. As they were speaking, he said wait, there is an incoming call to one of untraceable phones that was used earlier; as usual, it is jumping signals. Let me patch it to your phone as well, so that you could hear the conversation sir. Well do that and he disconnected the phone.

In a matter of seconds, his phone rang and he took the phone and silently listened to the conversation.

Yes! Brandon, how can I help you?

Do you have any information for me before I take my next step?

The person on the other hand, knew that it was a game that Brandon was playing as to confuse Leonardo before he took the next leap.

As a matter of fact, Yes! I do, they are currently in Turkey looking for you. They caught you on one of the surveillance cameras in a car store and they have started in Turkey, by all probabilities, he should be there in Turkey now.

But this time, Brandon could hear a changed voice as if the voice is manipulated this time just to make sure that person believes that someone else is hearing the call. Brandon didn't panic and didn't want the receiver to be alarmed that he found that out.

Right! Do you think we can meet tomorrow? Say between 1100 and 1300 hours in the morning. There is a nice coffee shop in a hotel called Royal Gateway, slightly far, but it will be worth a ride.

Of course, let's meet and I think it's time too.

Both Brandon and the mystery caller knew that they are trying to fake it as they wanted to stop Leonardo for a long time; and they know that both of them are not going to turn up as time is of the essence.

And they disconnected the line.

After hearing the conversation, Leonardo smiled and said they think they can fool me over and over again. But this time my friend, I'm not falling into your bait.

He rose from his seat and said I wanted to know the place where Franco stayed and the route that he took with a hired cab the day before he was killed. Get me the details in the next one hour and let me know if there is anything particular in that journey that he made.

44

With every passing minute Leonardo could feel that his confidence is getting plummeted, but he didn't want to show the same to his people. He knew that the minute he puts his guard off, there are hundreds of people waiting to take him and get his place. But that was least of his worries.

Leonardo just wanted two things. 1) Understand what he has lost and try to retrieve it 2) Why is Ambra in Turkey, is it just because of her father or is there something more to the mystery that he is not sure of.

Whatever it was, this time Leonardo was ready.

Brandon was enjoying the show from a nearby location, something that Leonardo had not thought of. Brandon had Leonardo under surveillance and he is doing it personally this time to avoid all the confusion and lecture that he would have to do. But surveillance is a hard task and boring at times, because of lack of sleep and you will never know when your opponent would come out a building, sometimes it might take days. But fortunately for Brandon, he saw the door opening and Leonardo along with his gang walking out of the building and getting into a car.

He had some papers in his hand and Brandon was not able to take a good look on to that. He didn't worry much and Leonardo first went to the hotel where Franco stayed when he visited Turkey and there was a cab driver waiting for him. He got into the cab back seat while one of his men pulled out his gun and got into the front seat next to the driver. Showed the photograph and Franco and asked him do you remember where you took him. Shocked and baffled the driver just gave a nod. And that was enough for Leonardo. He said **drive.**

Without a second being wasted, the driver ignited the car and started driving through the same road where he took Franco, he didn't say a word, but the person sitting next to him understood that he wanted to say something. What is it? Spit it out.

This is going to be a long journey and I would presume that you are well equipped for the journey and hope you would…. And before he could complete his sentence Leonardo said that would be our headache and you just drive us to be place where you took him.

Leonardo's car was following the cab and in a distant but visible to Brandon and not vice versa, Brandon was also on the trail.

The only thing that Brandon is thinking is how to bug Leonardo permanently so that he would be able to understand every move and what he is trying to do. That is not going to be an easy roll of dice, there are going to be multiple permutation and combination. He wanted to fathom Leonardo's motive and understand what exactly he is looking for. And Brandon also had a clear idea as this would also reveal the place where he needs to start the search in order to get what he wanted. He was willing to risk his life in order to complete the mission, but at the same time, he also wanted to make sure that Ambra is safe.

As he was following the car, he got a call. He took the phone and saw it was from Kevin. He answered using his Bluetooth and was on speaker as talking while driving would get deviated from the actual task and he wouldn't be able to keep a good look at the road and dangers ahead.

Where are you?

Following Leonardo, to the place where Franco went for the last time. And I sure do hope that is it, but only time will tell.

What are we supposed to do in the mean time?

Two things 1) try to think of a way to get a bug at least a listening device if not video on Leonardo for good. 2) Pacify Ambra and let her know that I'm ok and get her to safety if need be.

I will be reachable on this number, if I don't answer your call for 3 times in a row I'm either abducted or killed. If neither of this is happening, I hope to be back in the hotel and would join you guys for dinner.

45

A glass of scotch dropped from Kevin's hand as he heard an unexpected knock on the door at 5:00PM. He was cautious to open the door and he held out a gun while he unlocked and at the same time Brandon also cleared his leather as he didn't expect that.

You scared the devil out of me bud.

I intended to; said Brandon with a smile.

Drinking early?

Yeah, didn't have much to do other than thinking how to plant that bug, but all the roads were coming to the same conclusion, either I would be dead trying or would be dead thinking. Either way, I end up dead.

Sounds like a plan to me said Brandon jokingly.

You seem to be in a good mood and, May I ask why, as Ambra came into the room from hers. She was in a bathrobe and Kevin couldn't stop staring, while

Brandon was trying his best to act as everything is normal.

Well we also need to provide a treat to our eyes as well at times, said Kevin loudly and which made Ambra to nod her head and walked to her room and get herself changed.

And now if you could please answer me, why are you sounding to be in a good mood or are you?

Actually a part of me is asking for the party, because, I found the route from here to the place where we can be very close to the treasure. But...

I knew it, there would be a 'but' coming; Kevin interrupted.

Spit it

It would take us very... But that's all the driver knows, he also knows that he had a trekking gear packed and he used it to climb the mountain, he started early and was back by evening and he has no idea where he went and what he did from the time he dropped Franco near that mountain until he returned.

Now, we have a place to start looking for that, but we need to do that peacefully, Leonardo should be out of the picture completely and we need to make sure that we give him the death that he deserves.

Leonardo on the other hand was wasting time trying to think where he would have possibly gone from there and he was deviating from the actual reason why he was in Turkey. Until someone intervened and asked him, what is our next move on Ambra? The question broke his thought flow and said they need to be out of the picture and we need to have what they have only then we can take this forward; but at this time, it is slightly unclear as to how we are going to do it.

This is the first time in his lifetime that he got an enemy who has the power to give him a ride of his life and he didn't like it.

So it was up to him to give it a jerk and bring it to an end. But only one issue remained, where to start.

He knew that it was Brandon who lured him to Turkey, he started walking back and forth multiple times before he said every time he is one step ahead of us, are you sure that he doesn't have anyone who is helping him from within or from outside. He won't be able to pull this show together just by two of them, I want to know the details of his phone calls, his past friends, his associates in both fields or work and otherwise. I need to know anything and everything about him and it's time that we brought in someone to get the details and he owes me a lot. Let me see, if I can get hold of him.

Who is it? Asked one of his members; when it's time you will know and I don't think that time will come in this lifetime of yours. Sometimes my friend, ignorance is bliss.

46

There are quite a few things that we need to finish and time is in essence the more we delay, the more the probability of Leonardo finding us. It came to my attention that he also has resources at very high places and not to talk about the gadgets that he possesses. So, let's not be too hasty and waste the time in our hand. We need to come up with a plan and we need to plan it quick, we need to lure the rat out of his hole and take him because it won't be wise for us to fit ourselves through the rat hole and taking him there. Every man is a king in his own domain and in case we do that, it would be suicidal. So we need a plan said Brandon.

Ambra nodded in agreement and we need to come up with one very fast. As far my understanding goes, we need to get Leonardo in a place where we seem fit and take him there and then go behind what dad wanted me to see.

Kevin rose from his seat and said Planning is very important, but at the same time it is not easy to come up with one. How are we going to lure him to a place where we want.

Now what do we have? Brandon asked

What do you mean? Kevin said

We have a criminal mind with a cop brain coupled with that could give us results. And he has a criminal mind with a criminal brain, but at the same time we cannot think that he is lower than us, he would definitely have more resources and more influence at this point of time than all of us combined; Which means, we need to use our brains as a greatest weapon which should be deadly enough to face all kinds of music on the way.

We can do this, but we need a full proof plan. Primarily, we know that he is looking for us to get to the bottom of this and we can do this by making ourselves visible to him, we need to have a fully orchestrated appearance and the bad news is that we don't have time to practice, we learn, master the timings in our head and action; nothing else in between.

Ambra could feel butterflies in her stomach, learning from what they say and not many things get repeated them, they teach, this is going to be a hard ball in my court.

Brandon volunteered to be the bait for Leonardo, which gave Ambra some breathing space, which didn't last long.

While I'm doing my public appearance, you would have to watch Leonardo and give me an update every time and all of us would be connected to a call at the same time and we are going to be the eyes and ears for each other.

How are you planning on doing that? Inquired Ambra.

Good question, I'm going to take a room in the Royal Gateway hotel and appear myself in a couple of surveillance cameras. I just hope that he has not given up his search on us, though the cameras in the locality; I'm going to be there all the time until he or his men shows up. In case his men are coming without him, give me the word and I would be a ghost that they cannot find.

We are with you Kevin and Ambra said that in unison and they looked at each other and smiled.

Ambra, please pose as my secretary Tammy and make a reservation in the Royal Gateways Hotel.

In the mean time, Leonardo on the other hand was trying to get the details of the people and as Brandon suspected, he had influence at very high levels.

He took his personal mobile phone, dialed a number and waited for someone to pick it up.

He waited for 5 rings to get completed and when the phone was answered he said "The rabbit is out of the hat" and disconnected the call.

47

After a while as Leonardo was resting in his room a man came out of his toilet, well as a matter of fact, I can see why you should be disturbed especially when Brandon Brookes is on your trail. Leonardo turned back to see who it is.

He handed over a file to Leonardo and said this file contains disks, papers and all information about Brandon Brookes and also along with is attached his known associates and close friends.

What about any next to kin or known relatives? I would have to say none sometimes even the best force in the country would have to be in shame as not all information are available. We have no idea about his family, his parents, next to kin or if any relatives. As a matter of fact, we don't have his juvenile records. What we have managed to source is there in that file.

You may have connections with the CIA, but that doesn't help to get all information.

Care for a drink and Leonardo turned to the shelf; as he didn't receive an answer, he turned back and his friend from the CIA has vanished and not to be seen in that room.

Man! Talk about ghosts and I need to learn that kind of thing, the CIA way, Leonardo thought to himself.

He opened the file and with every passing page, he was getting impressed and getting scared at the same time. Brandon Brookes in Armed Forces, nothing can be compared to him, 100% success rate in all the operations that he has commanded; a very special rare breed. His trainings were the most effective. His known associates and his friends were equally impressive in their own areas of specialty. And as the pages in that file came to an end, the last page of that file contained the information about Kevin, the multi billionaire who served in the Police department as a Detective.

He asked his men to run his name across their database, Kevin O'Connell. And in a matter of minutes he had the information on his finger tips. The best ever success rate in the industry across the US and also at the same time hailing from a wealthy family; last case handled, Suspicious missing turned homicide of Franco Gallo. And that very moment, Leonardo could feel the mud under his legs been washed away. He sat down in a nearby chair and lit his favorite cigar and closed his eyes.

Everything is making sense now, Leonardo said with his eyes closed.

They were behind Franco, trying to understand his whereabouts and what he is up to, Ambra took Brandon's help to give a kick start to their journey. Brandon a good friend of Franco, who was willing to provide his helping hand and expertise to his daughter; to find him and bring him back home.

Brandon decided to get Kevin also on that trip as he is the last person who has investigated her father's missing, which after good long years turned to be a suspicious homicide. Coincidence at its best, Franco good friend to Brandon and Kevin another friend to Brandon -> all of them under the very same umbrella and fighting against their common enemy... ME.

But only the fittest will survive and who decides the fit, us and no one else.

The one piece that I'm not able to put together so far is how did they manage to get what was rightfully mine, the one that Franco destroyed when one of my own made sure that he rests in peace.

Brandon, with his computer skills created a plenty of ghost networks when I was trying to access Franco's system. Did he keep a copy of that, if so, we should be able to track that down again?

We need to try to get back on his system and try to access it, as Brandon is now here, we may have time to get that done. Try and access all the contents in that computer at Franco's house in Utica. We need to get our hands on.

His team was on that trying to get into that system, but before Brandon left the house, he has unplugged all the cables running to that computer so that an outside force cannot get into that computer and they need to be in that house to plug it and get the search going.

Leonardo receives a phone call and he was told that – the cables are unplugged and they need someone in that house to get those plugged to get on to that computer. Leonardo arranged that within a matter of minutes and with one phone call, there were more than ten people lined up near the Franco's house in Utica to plug the computer back into the network.

48

What are you thinking now Brandon? Ambra pondered.

I just said that Leonardo has a criminal brain with a criminal mind.

Yes! That you did. What about it?

If he was so brilliant, he should have understood that Franco had made the copy of what he is looking for and it should be stored in his computer and that's how we would have got it, rather than coming behind us, why can't he look for that in your place and I sure if your father was followed, he should know where he lived as well.

You got a point there, but even if he did search, how we will come to know until and unless we are back home to find the house tossed.

Ambra said you are right Kevin, how will we come to know about that from here when they are doing the search back there.

Brandon smiled.

Kevin said oh! No, you didn't do what I think you did.

Yes! I think you got half of it, but not a full picture.

So what did you do Brandon?

A lot of things, in fact. To start with the motion sensors; the place now is crawling with motion sensors and I would get a signal if anything or anyone is inside the house who is 4 feet or taller. I didn't want to keep it on the ground otherwise; I would be getting false alarms all the time.

Secondly, there is a brand new automated gadget that I have fixed on all the walls in the entire house.

What does that do? Ambra asked in surprise.

That is the best thing ever, it's just a prototype for the time being, it will detect any kind of radiation from a cell phone inside the house and it would clone the device with another one that I have set there in less than 1 minute and I would get the information in my personal computer as soon as the cloning is over and all we have to do is, create a virtual phone on my computer and we can operate using just a headset and mic, the clone would provide us with all the contacts, messages, videos, photos everything on that phone.

That's really nice. Ambra said in a shocking tone.

That's not even half the picture. Once the clone is complete, it would send a signal to that phone and that phone would be in our control to make or drop calls and more importantly, any call that comes to that phone or goes out of that phone, the receiver's phone also would be infected with a small virus that I created irrespective of the type of the phone they are using and the same would be cloned for our usage.

We would be able to listen into their conversations, add our bit of dialogue in according to one of the voices during that call, and make sure the phone is switched off or switched on anytime. Once all the cloning is complete, we would also get hold of Leonardo's phone for sure and once the entire procedure is complete, we would be controlling his entire move how we want it from where we want it.

And the best part is that, once the whole course of action is complete, I can replicate everything that is on my computer to my cell phone and I would be the person who would be handling everything within a click of a button on my phone, I wouldn't have to carry my laptop everywhere I go.

Brilliant plan indeed said Kevin, but it's been days since we have left the US and still no sign of attack in her place.

Yes! I understand, said Brandon... What are the odds?

49

It is definitely a brilliant plan Brandon, but if they enter our house, they would get the map don't you think that would be a pretty risky affair?

I do, and that's the reason why I thought about it before I left your place. I have primarily deleted that file and they won't be able to recover it even with the best recover tool that they might have and secondly I had to get them to your house because in today's technology anybody with the right skills would be able to access any computer across the globe if it's connected to a network and the very smart would give them hundreds of ghost servers to search before they actually land up on the right one. So this is what I did, the minute your computer goes online, thousands of ghost servers would be connected and they wouldn't be able to pin point the right computer for at least an hour and that would give me enough time to clone the phones in your house and most importantly if they have to get to your computer, they need to be in your house because I have unplugged all the cables from the computer and it would take another 3 to 5 minutes before your computer goes online and I would get a signal from the time they open your front or back door and if they chose to come from the top even better, that would give us more than 5 minutes before your computer comes online.

Smart move; Ambra's eye brows raised as that impressed her a lot.

If that had happened, luring them to a place where we can set a trap would have been easy, but with that being said we need come up with a plan B; at this point of time my mind is empty. What do you think guys any prospects?

Just as he finished that sentence his computer started to beep, Brandon was happy to see that and he switched on the computer and said guess they read my mind, his gang of members are in your house at this time and the phone cloning of 20 of his associates are in progress give it another 40 seconds and we would have their phone details with us and I'm sure one of them would definitely try to contact his team of tech experts and while another one who would try to contact him and we would be able to get what we wanted at this time.

And I also hope that the tech experts phone is currently connected to a computer for feeding purpose if so my virus would also attack their computer network I would be able to access and see what he is accessing at any given point of time in my ipad and things would be more easy that we think it would be.

I'm glad!

Brandon turned back to his computer to see the progress and he could see all the phone in that house are cloned and the minute he was about to check one of them, a call was in progress from another and he switched on the speakers so that everyone could listen to the conversation.

The person on the other end answered the call.

Alright now, we have plugged the computer back in and what next. He understood that the receiver is a tech expert's the way he was helping the other person. Brandon opened another computer and logged into that one with a key. He punched in some letters and numbers and all Ambra and Kevin was to hear the punching sound of the keys on his keyboard and on the monitor he could see what the tech people were seeing at that point of time.

Thank you lord, Brandon said. The virus has cloned the techie's phone and computer and now we are able to see what they see and what they hear.

Dear Lord, he has created thousands of ghost servers and it would take some time before we actually find the right computer that we have to search. He called Leonardo from his phone unknowing about the attack on his phone and computer and totally unaware that there are others listening to this conversation.

He informed Leonardo about the situation and it is going to take some time to find the right computer and would be some time before we could find what we are looking for as that is a wild goose search as we don't know what we are looking for.

Alright! Keep me posted and it doesn't matter, I will ask the boys to search the house as well and then leave the premises.

He called one of his associates in the house and told him to search every corner of that house and to let him know immediately if found something relevant. And if not, make a list of all the items in that house, take a few photographs probably my tech team or myself would be able to find something out of the ordinary. Once you are done with all that, leave the premises immediately.

Brandon on the other hand was tapping something on his computer and Kevin intrigued.

He said I'm trying to get into their digital cameras as well, I wanted to make sure that I erase all the photographs the minute they leave the building because sometimes, it would be something that we have thought about would give them a lead and they would be ahead of us and that cannot be permitted or made possible. So give me some time, let me see if I can figure this out.

50

After a good 4 hour search they left the premises in Utica and they made a call to Leonardo. We searched every nook and corner of the house and didn't find anything useful. And they knew his anger so they were very subtle in telling him that the camera that they had didn't work and as a matter of fact they were carrying only one. But we are uploading the photos on the computer that we took from the place, certain photos are not clear but I'm sure we can make it right. We are sorry.

Even though Leonardo was angry, he just disconnected the phone; waited for the photos to be uploaded.

Brandon on the other hand was trying hard to modify every picture that they took from the back end, he didn't want the right pictures, but instead he uploaded the pictures of Franco's earlier home in Utica before they moved into their new house.

Leonardo waited patiently until the photos were downloaded and he started going through one by one. Some of them as mentioned were not clear but the others were of no use either. He was stressed and frustrated. He didn't know what to do.

He turned to the tech team and what do we have by now? Do we have anything solid?

Yes! To start with we found the right computer and we are currently going through all the files that is there and the ones they have deleted. But until now we have no luck in tracing anything useful and this would take slightly longer as we have to open each and every file to see and understand if it means something and more importantly we are not sure ourselves what we are looking for.

Let me make it easier for you. Try something with Turkey in this or any place that is located in Turkey anything and everything scan it and probably even if it's the smallest thing that doesn't matter very much to you, keep a tab of it and let me know, I will be back in an hour.

Leonardo took a car and signaled his guys not to follow him and they obliged. They knew if anything important happens they would get their signal on their phones and then they would have to reach where he is and there is a dedicated team to help them locate Leonardo's location within seconds.

Leonardo went to a coffee shop and then he took his phone and called his girl friend.

And Amy answered the call. Hi Amy

Leo what's up long time, are you back?

No I'm still in Turkey. I'm really stressed and I could use some nice voice and I called you. You can call me anytime sweetie pie.

What's brooding you Leo; anything that I can help with?

Nothing, it's the same old story and the same old guy. Are you still using that old phone of your? Because I'm having a hard time hearing you.

No! Problem, do you want me to call you back? Not required Leo, go ahead.

What is that I can do sitting across the globe and I cannot even give you a hug to warm you up. But nevertheless, here is a kiss for you to make things work.

Brandon along with Ambra and Kevin were listening to that call. And when they hung up, Brandon just smiled.

51

B randon said I think I know who that lady is.

What's the big secret in that, her name is Amy; we all listened to that right now. Ambra said without thinking.

No Ambra, I think I know Amy that's what I meant. It's just a hunch, but maybe I'm wrong.

Why don't you give it a try, what if? Said Kevin

I'll be right back; Brandon took his phone and headed out

As soon as he closed the door behind him, he took his phone and dialed a number.

It was an automated voice again at this point of time, like the receiver suspects a call monitoring in progress.

Why do you keep calling me?

Brandon said I think it's time for us to meet and I know that you are here in Turkey even though you fooled us by saying you are on the other side of the globe. The receiver smiled and I think it is time for us to meet too.

In that case, our usual place in 30 minutes?

And they mutually agreed on the time.

Place: Royal Gateways coffee shop

Brandon ordered for a coffee and was waiting for the unseen but familiar caller to come in. He was reading the news paper just to kill time and also to hide his face from the rest of the people in the room, just in case as an added precaution.

A minute later a beautiful woman walked by and asked him, is this place taken? Brandon without moving his news paper that hides his face said No, you can sit if you like; he also added, I will meet you in the red car outside the coffee shop and sitting here and talking is not good, you will never know who will recognize you or me.

So finish your coffee and I will see you outside. He paid the bill that was already on the table and took off.

Few minutes later, there was a tap on the window of Brandon's car. He opened the door and let her in and started to drive the car. Now let's talk… Amy.

How did you find my name and my number and how are you tracking me. I was very careful all the time.

Yes! You were. It's not your phone but Leonardo's phone was getting monitored by me and gave up your location as well. I knew you were cooking something, the minute the location was nailed to Turkey and you said I would have given you a hug, but I'm half way across the globe. What gave you up is your voice. Without anyone knowing, I actually ran your voice in an application that I have developed to understand the right voice in case the caller is using an automated voice changer and your voice was recognized. My associates back in the room still don't know who you are or what you do, it was just a hunch even for me and I thought I would try my luck.

Amy smiled and said I think it time for you to know who I'm and why I'm trying to help you. Yes! As a matter of fact, I would like to know everything.

Mike was Leonardo's most trusted henchman, his right hand at all times. Mike was my brother too. He would do anything that Leonardo asks him to do and sometimes a lot more. He always says that he wants to get out of that life and leads a nice life some place where Leonardo wouldn't be able to use him. He wanted out, but he never talked about this to Leonardo or me. I just thought that's what he wanted from his face.

To cut the long story short, Mike is the person who killed Ambra's father. But not out of his will but he had no choice. Franco attacked Mike and the gun fired. He was not able to retain what Franco knows, because Franco burned the paper that he had with him. I guess that was very important to Leonardo.

When he got back to Brazil, he told Leonardo what has happened, but he didn't believe his most trusted lieutenant that has ever served him. Tyrannical that he is, he didn't waste much time and put a bullet on his head. It was a devastating moment for me. Not that I lost my only family but I didn't even get to see his body, Leonardo made that disappear without a clue.

I started to follow him and gave appearances as it was an accident and he fell for it. We have been seeing each other for the last 2.5 years now; today he trusts me too.

Recently I came to know that you along with Ambra and Kevin are searching for Franco and wanted to see what Franco saw and you have the copy of the paper that Franco burned down before he died. So I thought enemy to a common enemy make us friends; more importantly I could give you clues and other guidance to help you proceed further when I feel that you are stuck.

Not here after, we can talk to each other anytime that you deem fit and we can take this to a next level and before we all know it, I want this to end too; tears were rolling down her cheeks as she finished.

Brandon heard all of this in one breath and without taking his eyes of the road. He gave a sign on relief and the same time; he knew it is going to be hard to make Ambra understand why Amy is helping us.

Amy, as we mutually understand that it would take a life time to make Ambra realize your intentions because she would only see you as the sister of the person who killed her dad. So to make sure that we reach our goal I think that this information should not be revealed to her until everything is over.

I agree said Amy.

52

We scanned each and every file on this computer. Most of it was junk, some bank statements, yearend turnover statements and things like that. Nothing related to Turkey or related to any places here in Turkey.

We even searched the deleted files and tried to recover what was recently deleted, nothing. That computer was clean. Not sure if we have any other computer in that house. Like a laptop or a different CPU.

No. We searched that house top to bottom and nothing turned out to be useful there either.

There was one file that stood from the rest of it and we have kept a print out for you. They handed the print to Leonardo. It read "I've got you".

Leonardo understood that it was from Brandon and he just smiled. He said I think now we don't have to do anything, we will be contacted and I guess we would get what we want at the earliest. And nothing can stop us now. We just need to wait for the time being.

But with that being said I don't want to stop searching for them.

Remember, we have received information about Kevin in that file that I handed over to you. Could you check for his face in any of the surveillance videos where we came across Brandon and Ambra from the time that they left US and also check to whom that Private Jet is registered to; as we had a couple of Private Jet scheduled during that time frame when Brandon was in Brazil.

Kevin was there in every place where Brandon was seen including here in Turkey.

That confirms my doubt and now I know how they all played along. He had one face that we didn't look for and he played us nicely; that helped him to be one step ahead of us all the time. But not anymore, we need to make sure that he doesn't get away this time.

Our facial recognition software is still running at the Airport and other connected surveillance feeds right.

Yes!

Good, keep that running and I want them to be found at the earliest.

In the mean time every member of his team was calling each other to understand the gravity of the situation and to figure out the whereabouts of Brandon. And with each and every phone call, each of their phones was getting cloned in the backend without their knowledge and every conversation was getting recorded by Brandon.

Brandon was recording every conversation so that it might help him to get an idea to get Leonardo where he wanted him and take him.

Brandon had made up his mind that a person who is wanted by almost all the forces across the globe. Death is what should be waiting for him and nothing else, if Ambra is not able to do it, I would. And that's the least that I could do for a friend.

53

Amy, another thing, what can you tell me about Leonardo and his family. Any small detail would help me finalize a plan that can lure him to a place that I want rather than taking one step at a time; I would love to take him once and for all.

Not much I would say, but I can share the information that my brother has shared with me but my memory on those little matters may not be what you think it is. Anyways, Leonardo's grandfather was British, they came to Brazil long time ago, at that point of time, and we had a lot of people who were coming to different parts of our country looking for Gold. Building tunnels and trying to mine, they tried different ways to find the valuables. But unfortunately none of them succeeded. At that point of time, Leonardo's grandfather found an opportunity to make easy money. They needed a place to stay, buy things that they require to proceed with what they came looking for and they needed water and food. That was the opportunity that he found.

He opened up a motel, a hardware store, a liquor store and everything that a traveler required. His business flourished. Even though the people who came to town looking for different kinds of priceless stone ended up paying Leonardo's grandfather money for the services he rendered. And that was not enough, when the money started to accumulate; he got into trafficking of women from different places to accommodate those wild dreams of the travelers. When that business was brought into the marker, he was more known among the locals as the inn keeper. To make sure that he stays out of all trouble, he started to hire the local thugs to take care of the unwanted visitors to his inn.

When the travelers stopped coming to down as it spread that there is no valuables in our town, his business started to reduce and so did his income. Later he moved to selling women to the people around the globe, which got him connections and influence at very high level. Later he moved into drugs, smuggling of human body parts and arms & ammunition.

Money, fame and influence came into their family. Later before he left his body, he named his clan the Carunio's.

They started killing each and everyone who stood in their way, ruthlessly, taken the life of many, leaving their wife's, kids and family alone. And to feed all those stomach's they either sell their flesh or those who didn't want that to happen, they killed themselves.

Coward selfish act as some people call it, but what can a human life do, if all the doors of opportunity shuts in front of them one fine morning. There is a level of stress that each one of us can take but not necessarily everyone is courageous enough to face the day to day life. If you ask me those are not an act of selfishness, that is bravery not everyone can take their life into their own hands.

Anyways, Carunio married from a very wealthy family. The word of the street is the Ghost. He met his pair in the darkest corners of Brazil and they had a son, Leonardo.

He was brilliant and unlike other Carunio's he had an individual thinking process, the most cruel, cold blooded human that I have ever come across. Brilliant and intelligent, has a master's degree in various subjects. He is a perfectionist when using guns or any kind of weapons. His aim has not failed him ever, has completed karate training.

With all that said if he was in the streets as a normal guy, he would be the most eligible bachelor in town.

This is what I know about his family. Nothing more and nothing less.

Thanks, this should help me formulate a plan to get things in action.

Brandon stopped the car and dropped of Amy from the same place he picked her up.

He rolled down the windows and said. Amy, don't you ever think that you have nobody to give you a shoulder to lean on.

Turned back, wore his sun glasses and sped away.

While Amy smiled and followed him with her beautiful eyes until the car was out of sight.

54

Brandon returned to their hideout. Where were you Ambra cried out loud, you had me worried, it's been hours since you been out and you are breaking the rules set by you.

I'm sorry, I was out and I had to be alone to think of a way to get things in shape.

And did you?

As a matter of fact, I did and I have a plan. But before that, let me just freshen up and we will all go out for a nice juicy steak dinner and I will outline the plan with you guys.

And heads up, don't be scared and trust me on this one.

Hours later, they all returned back. Kevin said Are you sure that this is gonna work? If not, we all are in trouble. Ambra said... Trouble? Are you kidding Kevin – We all would be dead if one of us makes a slightest mistake.

As I said guys, trust me on this one.

Do we have a choice?

Brandon smiled and said we absolutely do, if you can come up with anything better.

Give us time till day break, let me analyze this plan and see if there are any loop holes or things that might get us in trouble and also think of something else.

Alright! Then, let me call it a day. Very tired and will see you in the morning.

Rise and shine, let me have a coffee, does anyone else apart from me want a coffee, I'm planning room service.

Na! not me said both Ambra and Kevin in unison and they looked at each other and smiled. Brandon just shook his head and called Room service.

In a matter of minute, his coffee was delivered and mixed it well. And now tell me what do you guys think of my plan. It's kind of risky but doable. I tried to think of various other plans that originated from your initial idea but all of them took the same path and showed me the exact same ending.

And that would be, inquired Brandon.

In a nice cozy coffin.

As a matter of fact, my plan also would end up there, if we deviate from the plan but we can definitely improvise to the situation, going by the gut feeling, but we need to make sure that we trust our inner feelings and things would work.

Faith and that's all we need to have at this point of time. We can do this and we definitely will.

Are you all in favor?

Kevin and Ambra looked at each other and said Thumbs up and we are ready and Ambra lowered her voice and said

I think.

55

Leonardo was waiting for a plan to get better of Brandon and Kevin, but he was not getting a starting point. He is now thinking of a plan to get one step ahead of him rather than capturing him. Only if he is able to think like him, he would be able to do it and then capture him and tell him a tale.

A tale about a Ex-armed personal tried to get better of him before he could break all the bones in his body. But nothing is happening at this point of time, I think, said one of the gang member in a conversation, while Leonardo was resting in his room.

Leonardo without knowing any of this was trying to analyze every situation from the very beginning and was retracing his movements and trying to understand a pattern. There is always a pattern and that's how these armed personals are trained. They can just improvise but never deviate from the plan. Now that's what kept Leonardo thinking why he took the help of Kevin.

Understanding more about Kevin, he had an answer for that the billionaire rich kid with a private jet and enough and more money to squander which he inherited and who else is better than the person who was a detective and the last case was about Franco.

He was jotting down everything, the minute detail of the scenes, the movement and everywhere were Brandon's presence was felt, Kevin was there right beside him, probably not close, probably watching from a distant view and I guess Brandon's appear in front of the camera was not accidental, that was a plan to get me here.

Leonardo was getting closer and his phone rang by breaking his flow of thought.

Leo! Who is this? He answered the call.

Your worst nightmare.

My worst nightmare, you got to be kidding my friend, I may be a nightmare to million people to but to give me a nightmare, your standards are not enough and you should know by now that I'm not easily shaken, if this is not a joke.

Oh! I know that. You are not easy shaken but you are easily frustrated when you cannot think straight.

Who is not frustrated, when one is not able to think straight? Now cut the chase and tell me who am I talking to?

This is Brandon and I guess you are looking for me?

Leonardo was taken aback.

How the hell did you get my number, especially, when my number cannot be tracked?

I have my resources and you were a bit over confident that your number cannot be traced and I know where you currently is and what you are doing, you have been under my radar all the time.

Brandon being a master in poker, he could bluff and easily get away with it.

Ha! That's a joke, you of all people should know that this number cannot be traced.

Well, what if I tell you, your current location and then take it from there so that I can earn your trust and you could do the listening.

Leonardo was terrified for a moment there, but that was not enough to pull him along.

Forget the location where I'm talking to you from, tell me which all locations did this call skip.

Not sure what you are talking about. Let me tell you this, you are using an old school phone so that, you cannot be tracked using the GPS and you would be thinking, as your signals are jumping from Australia to Thailand and across the continents, I cannot give an exact trace. You should be something else.

I'm something else, I can be your friend and you would like it and if I change colors not even the Gods can save you from that wrath.

You are talking from your bedroom and I have you on my sight and when I have you on my sight, why should I even rely on the computers that keep telling me that your signals are jumping. Brandon bluffed. If he was in an open area, the wind would have made it difficult to hear and if were with his gang, I could have sensed it by other sounds in the background. And that concluded, he is in a closed space and if my feelings serve me right, it has to be his bedroom. So Brandon gave it a shot.

Where are you talking to me from?

Brandon knew his bluff worked.

From nearby so that I can keep you in surveillance myself rather than depending on people.

Now that I have your attention, what is that you want?

Leave it here, stop following me.

I would have done that, if you haven't gone behind this case and more important, you shouldn't have left US and come here looking for what was there in the map and I understand that you have deciphered it.

I most certainly have and Ambra would have left you alone if you hadn't killed her father and nothing of this sort would have happened.

I have no regrets and bygones are bygones.

You need to be ready to face the music for all the things that you have done and there would be no looking back.

What is that you want otherwise?

Let us be free and you don't need to follow us, we are not investigating the murder of Franco Gallo anymore.

I know you are not. And even if you did, it wouldn't bother me. But I'm after you for what you have learnt from that piece of paper that was lost from me. And I want it back as I'm the rightful owner of whatever that you may find.

Nobody is... finders' keepers... Losers weepers; I don't have any intention to lose this game.

Neither do I.

56

Ambra and Kevin were listening to that conversation. Did he achieve what he intended?

I'm not sure Kevin said but one thing is for sure, now that we have his unbiased attention. And I guess that is our leverage and starting point.

I sure do hope, I have a feeling that this might end up in a bad shape.

I've that feeling too as for the last few days; Brandon has been keeping information from us. For example, we still don't know how he came up with this plan and more over where he was for a very long time.

I know Brandon for ages now and we have always been safe under his radar. Probably this is the first time he is divulging the full plan and that's what makes me wonder.

Ambra interrupted, don't be, if my father can trust him with his life, so can we. I'm sure and more importantly, he is doing this for me as there are no personal vendettas for Brandon against Leonardo. He is putting his life in line for me. I'm sure we all will come out of this alive.

Yes! You may be right there, but what we have in store at the end of this is much bigger than anything at stake and we are not sure what we are going to find. There is a devil sleeping inside all of us and you will never know when he would wake up and give us a shout.

Ambra thought for a minute and said there may be a devil, but again, if my father would trust him, I would do without any doubt, I will have full faith in him, even if the world ends with me, I will still believe him.

I do too.. Anyways whatever it is, only time will tell.

Leonardo on the other hand got panicked and said I need a new SIM Card, preferably a local SIM and only a handful of people would have my number. I need this as soon as possible.

We are getting you one, saying that some people just left the building.

Sometime later, they returned with a new SIM Card.

Write this number on a piece of paper and give it to me. And I will tell you who all needs to have this number, until then nobody gets it.

Leonardo came outside of his house and in his garden; he sat and started changing the SIM card on his phone. The minute the phone was switched on, it rang and it said Private Number Calling.

Who is this?

The voice said your nightmare with a smile. Did you really think, by changing the SIM card, I wouldn't have your number. You are thoroughly mistaken. My resources are better than yours and more importantly, you are just a filthy crook and a murderer and nothing more. On the flip side, I'm the good one and you have all the reasons to be annoyed at this point of time.

Brandon could sense the anger through the phone.

No worries, Leonardo, we will soon meet and then you can take the anger on me, leave your teeth alone else you won't have any to have some meat next time.

Where are you calling me from? You have no idea what I'm capable of. And you don't want to have an enemy like me and he disconnected the phone.

He went inside the house and said this is a new number and how did he get the information. Did you guys get a chance to run a trace on that call?

We tried, but it was jumping signals and we didn't have enough time to track it down to its location. The line was disconnected just in time.

But how did he get the number? Who else was in store when you were buying this connection?

No one, we made sure of that.

Then someone please tell me how?

Nobody has driven me nuts like these guys have and I'm surrounded by a group of baboons whose doesn't have brains to think of a plan. He is really annoying me and we don't have a starting point. Why am I paying such buffoons?

Leonardo stood there perturbed.

57

Kevin and Ambra joined Brandon on the roof of the hotel. Brandon smiled and said now its time to take this to the next level.

This is the time that we have been waiting for frustrated and annoyed Leonardo and if we strike now, it would be great as currently his state of mind is dragging him places and he is not able to think of anything other than being frustrated and stressed.

We act now, we win.

Alright then, what are we waiting for? Asked Ambra.

Brandon just smiled.

Kevin, you already have the routes that the cab driver took Leonardo. Tomorrow, the very first thing that you are going to do is take the car and drive to that very spot and see if you can identify anything.

Kevin looked puzzled. Remember the map but don't carry it with you. Look for anything that you can compare with the map, anything at all. Hillside, markings, representations, trees, the way they are. Anything and everything and carry a camera and a portable USB video recorder, try to put that as your sun glasses so that it records in case you miss to take any photographic images, we can compare both and we can see if it means anything.

We are on the game now, let's not look back, our vision is forward. Let's do this.

Ambra and I will arrange a rendezvous with Leonardo tomorrow and we will be ready to take him. We do have a lot of limitations as we are going to do that in a public place. The minute we lure him out and have him alone, he will bleed and he will cry for some air. And I want Ambra to see things in action.

Just in case, if we are not back here by six in the evening, it means we have a problem. It can be you or it can be us. If it's us, do not wait for us. By 6:30pm, you should be ready to leave and make sure you are out of the country before anyone is on to you.

Just be courageous and things will fall in place. Destroy you phone and then run away. Don't make any contact, just run.

Kevin could feel his throat being dry and he gulped a full bottle of ice cold water in one breath.

Ambra was nervous and losing her boldness, but she didn't let it show.

Step 1 has been completed successfully, but what matter is completing Step 2 and let me remind you, we do not have a plan B to execute. So whatever it takes, however long that we need to wait, Plan A has to succeed and then we will celebrate back home.

So morning 6:00PM Kevin would leave us and would follow the trail, while Ambra and I are supposed to meet Leonardo by 1:30PM and leave the rest in God.

Kevin and Brandon took out the bag that they have and started to put all the weapons that they have in order and the wait started for the sun to rise.

58

Brandon and the duos didn't get the sleep that they required that night because of the stress and excitement that is going to be there from the moment the sun brings in the warmth of light and hope.

Kevin packed a bag with all the required things from basic trekking gear, guns and anti-venoms just to be on the safe side and Brandon handed over a phone to him and said use this phone in case of emergencies and in case, you feel threatened, toss your phone and keep this one.

Kevin left just when the clock said 6:00AM.

And then Brandon and Ambra waited for some more time. When it was 11 O'clock, Brandon called Leonardo again.

Leonardo picked the call in one ring and said – What is that you need this time?

I think it's time for us to meet. Face to face and you need to come alone.

Leonardo smiled and said I'm not scared to come alone but my dear friend, you have no idea whom you are messing with.

I never under estimate my opponent. That would make me weaker isn't? But if I get a hint a very small bit of doubt that you are not alone, this meeting would be called off and we both might never meet. And you would lose the opportunity too.

Alright! In that case, we can meet at…

Brandon interrupted and said we will meet the same place where you've suspected me to be there. We will meet at the Royal Gateways Coffee Shop. It's a public place and the least that we can think about is taking each other there in front of the public and not to mention the CCTV cameras. Are you ok with that?

He just smiled and said… Yes I'm

Great, meet you at 1:30PM sharp.

Brandon could hear his smirk through the phone as the line went dead.

Leonardo on the other hand started to give instructions to his associates

Brandon and I are going to meet today at Royal Gateways. I want you guys to be in a very safe distance and the minute I give you my command it shouldn't take you more than 5 minutes to reach the location and take him. I would either call you or text you. If my situation is much worse, I would look into the CCTV and would signal you and the Tech Team would be wired to that CCTV all the time and more importantly, the minute I signal, the Tech team would initiate the call and you shouldn't take more than 5 minutes to reach there as discussed.

Any questions?

The room went silent for some time.

Good! One other thing, you are not going to follow me in the cars that we have, I want you to follow me in different cars and in a very safe distance. I don't want any chance to be taken to give him a fright and throw him off. I want him to think that I'm alone. And let me play it his way for some time before we take him down.

59

Leonardo reached the coffee shop right on time expecting to find Brandon seated somewhere. He went to the lady who was standing by the door to show him to his seat. He went near her and asked her, do you have any reservation in the name of Brandon or Leonardo.

Yes! Please come with me and she made him sit near a wall and he was pleased with the location.

Brandon was watching this from a car that is parked outside and Ambra from a roof of a nearby building, she could see the gang is already very close the hotel and they are waiting for instructions.

Ambra called Brandon and updated him about the situation outside.

Once the call is over, he took his phone and punched in some numbers. And the phones that were cloned earlier came online. He chose all of them, except

Leonardo's phone and switched them to Airplane Mode jamming all the signals that could put his life on the line.

He walked inside and pulled a chair where Leonardo was seated, looked at Leonardo and smiled.

So we finally meet?

Yes! Said Brandon.

How did you get your hands on a copy of what was there with Franco, the original was destroyed by him?

Getting a copy was the easiest thing, deciphering it was the hardest.

You know what it says?

We all know and you are not going to know either. I'm not going to give it to you my friend.

Leonardo got angry. But let me tell you this, you are not fit to be in this game.

Oh! No No, you got it wrong, you are not fit to be in this game. It not only takes to be brave to play the game that you are playing. It also needs brains and you lack that. You don't have one. You could have hired some people that have brains to work for you. But really, you have a bunch of babbling buffoons and a baboon leading them all the way. Have a couple of master's degree doesn't prove that you have brains. You have something else placed in your head, but I'm sure they are not brains.

Leonardo got really pissed and felt really insulted.

What do you mean?

I mean what I said you have been chasing me for the last few weeks but not once were you ahead of me. A person who claims to be the most dangerous of all and we are even having a cup of coffee in a place of my choice and not yours. Poor you; you had no idea what we were doing and what will do to get you out. It took you ages before you could use your head and get our information, your so called techie friends were not even close in getting our details. They are good, oh! Very good in fact in telling you, sorry we cannot trace the signal as we didn't have enough time and the signals were jumping from one continent to another.

Leonardo pulled his phone out and started typing under the table so that Brandon wouldn't notice.

Why are you trying so hard? Why don't you take your hands from below the table and actually make calls. Let's see how many would come running to take me down.

Leonardo started to call one by one but got really irritated as all the phones were out of coverage area. He turned back to spot a CCTV camera, but they were seated in a position where you don't have a direct access to a CCTV camera as the small wall was hiding it from its sight.

You have planned it to its detail. I don't have anyone who is going to come all the way to line up and take you down. But I'm here and that's all it matters. Leonardo took a gun out from his jacket, which was already connected to a silencer and aimed it against Brandon from under the table.

Quietly stand up and nobody has to get hurt, we will go from here and will discuss things in peaceful environment.

Brandon changed his seating position and said I'm not going anywhere, if I have arranged the meeting; I will give you orders not the other way around. Brandon was nervous inside, but he didn't show that.

It won't take me long before I put you out completely and I will still walk out of the door unharmed.

And that's where you have mistaken Leonardo, do you think I would walk into this den without being prepared, you walk out that door alone, you would be a dead meat before you reach your car. Hope you get it.

Brandon changed his seating position again.

So which means, I need to have you with me if I have to get out and what if I take you as a hostage and we both walk out.

Brandon was getting impatient with this teetotaler sitting next to him.

All of a sudden, Brandon attacked Leonardo using his hands under the table, the first thing that he did was to lock the trigger using his index finger and using the other hand, and he dismantled the gun in matter of seconds and had all the pieces of the gun on top of the table.

Leonardo couldn't do anything as he was taken by surprise.

Do you have enough proof by now that you don't have any brains at this point of time? You are seriously something. Anger is not going to take you places. Never be over confident that your opponent is weaker than you. And you haven't learnt that lesson even when you were far behind in this race between us. Not once been ahead of me. When are you going to learn?

Now listen, listen carefully, I have close to twelve snipers pointing at you at this very minute. And you are going to follow my instructions from now on. Brandon paid for the coffee in cash.

We are going to stand up and walk towards the car; you will get into the driving seat of your car and would follow me. And don't you worry you will not have any dirty ideas while driving, I will take care of that.

They both walked out slowly.

Leonardo got into his car and the minute the ignition was on, Ambra got up from the back seat totally dressed up and with a gun in her hand pointing at Leonardo. Now you can follow that car. And before we start, you see this switch next to me, if you do anything nasty trying to escape, I will press this switch and your seat would blow up and don't worry, nothing will happen to your car only the interiors would be covered with blood… your blood. So remember, I don't need this gun to kill you, so just be patient and follow that car.

Brandon slowly pulled his car out of the driveway and Leonardo followed.

60

Leonardo's associates were waiting patiently, unaware of what's happening. And as per the CCTV footage, Leonardo and Brandon were leaving the coffee shop together and that didn't raise a red flag amongst the tech team who had kept them on surveillance from the time they were detected on CCTV, even though for some time they don't know what was happening behind that wall.

Hours after they left the hotel, the tech team tried to get Leonardo on his phone, but the phone was unreachable and that raised a red flag with them. His phone is never unreachable; even so, we would know exactly where he would be.

They tried to locate him through the GPS that is installed on his car and to their surprise that was offline. They tried to contact his associates who were patiently waiting in a safe distance from the coffee shop and all their phones were unreachable too.

On the tech team members, got out; took a car and went straight to the place where his gang was waiting for Leonardo's signal and informed them about the situation. They all looked at their phone and saw that majority of their phones were in Airplane mode. They cursed themselves for not checking and they turned it back on. Got into their cars and went separate ways to look for Leonardo.

Ambra was instructed to disable the GPS in Leonardo's car as soon as the information was passed to Brandon about the people waiting to take him out. Proper instructions were given to Ambra over the phone on how to deactivate the GPS without raising an alarm.

She did as she was instructed and opened the back door of the car to let herself in and to setup a small bomb under the driver's seat incase Leonardo tries to do anything funny.

Leonardo was taken to place in the outskirts of the city, which looked like a forest area, wild and dark.

He was tied to a tree while they decided what to do with him.

Brandon looked at his watch, time was 5:10PM and in less than 50 minutes he needs to at the hotel, else, Kevin would leave the place thinking we are in danger.

Brandon raised his head, looked at Leonardo right in his eyes and reached to all of his pockets and emptied them all.

His phone, his wallet and that can help his locate the whereabouts were taken and was placed inside his car and Ambra agreed to drive it back to the parking lot of the coffee shop, while Brandon would follow her and pick her from there and would head back to their place of stay.

Brandon then looked at Leonardo and said we are leaving you here like this and we will be back in the morning. And if you are still alive, we will talk and we'll continue this until you are dead. They tied his mouth, so that he can't scream.

Leonardo's face became pale.

61

Brandon and Ambra walked into their den. Kevin was waiting there with his things packed. He left a sigh of relief when he saw them walking through the door. What happened, he inquired? Things went just as we planned; tonight the entire gang of his associates would be going haywire in many directions to find him. He needs to have a lot of luck and a lot of help to get him out of his current situation. Brandon kept his computer on the table and connected them to the speakers. He then switched to live tracking of all the phones, so that he could get the latest updates of what they think.

Ambra and Brandon turned to Kevin, so what happened at your end?

I found the place, Kevin replied instantly and excited.

And?

Oh! The place is awesome, we would have to trek and climb a lot to get to our destination, I was just there at the base of that gigantic mountain, and I found the mountain with that being said I'm confused too. I probably might have found the right one with what I had in mind, but I can't be sure until you check it out. You are a master in this, not me.

Brandon loaded all the photographs and videos on to his computer and Kevin and Ambra peeped into the screen over Brandon's shoulders.

Kevin started explaining what each of the photographs meant and where it was taken from. After hours of hunting both in the internet and based on the photographs, Brandon stood up from his place and gave Kevin a handshake; said "Good Job buddy", you found the correct spot.

Kevin smiled and bit his lips in excitement.

They woke up slightly earlier than usual called room service and ordered food for the entire day. They packed everything and left where they have tied up Leonardo to find his condition. They asked to be careful because by now all the companions would know our faces and we don't. So any suspicion of being followed, being looked at; then raise a red flag, so all of us can stand for each other, Kevin said.

When they reached the place and as they were walking towards Leonardo, Brandon said Guys, I want to tell you something and when I say this, please give your full attention and think before any one of you react to this. I withheld this information from you for a few days now.

What is it, asked Ambra?

How did I come up with this plan to capture Leonardo and who helped me?

Brandon told the entire story about who the caller was on the other side and about their long drive and the chit chat they had. After hearing everything, Ambra started to cry. You got help from a lady whose brother killed my father.

No, Ambra, don't put it that way.

That's the only way I will put it, you took help from her and you didn't bother to tell us.

Don't do this to yourself, not now, we are so close to our target.

You want, what my father found out, you wanted the treasure. Go take it, I don't care.

Brandon took his hand and kept it on her shoulder and said I was talking about Leonardo, who is in our custody and not about the treasure. I don't want to take a peep into that as I'm least interested, I promised I would help you find the person who brought harm to your father and will make him pay. He is right here in this jungle or whatever this place is and you know that he is there, right around that corner.

Even then Brandon. He didn't let her complete the sentence, he said trust me on this one. Amy's brother killed your father accidently and not with any prior or personal vengeance. Trust me on that.

Ambra wiped her tears down and gave him a hug.

One other thing, if you are ok, I would wish to invite Amy to this party, she also has some beef with Leonardo for taking her brother's spirit and if both of you could unite and exercise on this together, it would be great and peace can be brought to both of your spirits. What say Ambra? Are you ok with that?

Ambra went and sat near Kevin, who was listening to the entire conversation. Kevin held Ambra's hand and gave a nod. Ambra looked at Brandon and said Yes! You can bring her in. She also needs to be a part of this.

Kevin rose and went to Brandon, took his hand and pulled him and hugged him and said I need to apologize, as I misread you, I knew that you have been withholding information from us, but I never knew that you will talk about that to us. I'm sorry, now I know you wanted us to be safe and think straight all the time. Sorry once again.

Hey! Kevin.. You know me and nothing can come between us.

Brandon got his telephone and rang her number. As usual, a computer sounding voice picked up the telephone. Brandon said Got him and you know where we are… Meet us there.

On my way… is that he could hear before the phone went dead.

The trio reached the where Leonardo was tied; they removed the tape that was there to close his mouth from screaming.

His eyes couldn't lie, he looked as if he knew he is going to die and with that look they started to understand that he has lost his faith and confidence completely.

Ambra asked, how does it feel to be on the other side of the table? Terrible, isn't it?

Leonardo didn't reply.

Well, you should know, Karma is there and she won't let go of you so easily. We are going to give you enough room to repent for your misdeeds and regret about the sins that you did in this life and if you have another one, be rest assured, we would have our too. And she smiled.

Kevin and Brandon sat on a log nearby and they could see that Leonardo is observing what they are doing and trying to give them an offer.

Kevin rose and said so Leonardo, you didn't answer the lady.

I don't have to answer anyone and sooner or later, dead or alive, I would be found and you would regret this decision that you are taking, beware hell would rage fire on you.

All of them smiled, that is where you had us wrong, you are never going to be found, but before you leave this life for eternity, and there would be a lot of surprises in store for you.

That's when Amy reached the location. Leonardo was shell shocked. Amy what are you doing here and how did you get here?

Brandon went and hugged Amy and looked at Leonardo, this is the part that I would say, Hey! There, here is your first surprise and pray this to be your last. Then Brandon laughed.

You should understand Kevin and I have no personal vengeance against you, but these ladies have and as we have promised, the revenge is theirs and we are here to make sure that it happens. Ambra's you know, what kind of revenge that she holds for you and in a way Amy and Ambra are connected, because, it's her brother who killed her father, for you and what did you do? You killed him for not getting the stuff from Franco; the stuff that you require.

And the worst of it all, you have no idea about the value of that piece of paper that you have lost. It's huge and Brandon went and stood near Leonardo and whispered, it is a treasure map and we have deciphered it.

So Amy, you were part of their plot of lure me here and get your revenge, if that was the case, why did you even sleep with me? Just to convince me that you love me?

Amy smiled and said every time when we were together, you were drugged and I made you believe that we have slept together, especially when nothing has happened. You were too easy to be taken; she smiled.

Kevin came to Leonardo, we know how cruel you were with people that you were enemies with and how cruel and cold blooded you are. You didn't even spare the people who worked for you because they didn't get what you sought.

So killing you would be the easiest thing that we can do to you, but you don't deserve a fast death, slow and steady, probably we can take enough and more days to kill you, slowly.

Leonardo didn't speak, but his face told them that he was scared and pleaded guilty.

62

B randon and Kevin were watching the ladies and that is the time they experienced that the wrath of a woman can be so brutal that their cruelty might last long.

They took off his shoes and shirt. Amy took out two nails from her bag and she placed it under the heel and when Leonardo was pushed on that, his scream was heard in the deepest corner of that jungle. She passed over another nail to Ambra.

She took that nail and made a pair of holes in his ears and tied both the ears together by pulling it behind the tree; both of them made normal scratches with those nails, but careful enough not to let go of his blood.

Once they made enough wounds on his chest and arm, Ambra took out her pepper spray and sprayed it all over the wound and his eyes. Leaving Leonardo in a lot of pain; Kevin and Brandon were shocked to witness this brutality.

They didn't know that, these two can be so dangerous, but of course they can be, especially when a loved one is taken from your life, the pain and the wound are never healed and space in their heart that never can be filled. And they possessed all the rights to be savage.

Both Amy and Ambra sat down for some time for the pain to subside, so that they could start again, Brandon could read their faces; their anger knew no bounds and they were not ready to talk.

Both Brandon and Kevin gave them their space. Brandon said Kevin and I would there near that lake and you would be able to see us, give us a shout and we would be back once you finish with him. We will think of a way to dispose his body.

They just nodded and gave them their concurrence.

They chose a wooden board and held it under Leonardo's feet and nailed the feet onto the wood, Leonardo knew that all his sins and curses are coming to an end, but this was not the time to repent, but to cry in pain.

Ambra said we are not going to do anything to your manhood because sometime in the future, you would be known as a man less creature with a manhood. Shame on him, he didn't have brains too, to be equal with his enemies A name that you can take to your grave and with that being said Amy pulled out a knife and popped one of his eyes out and poured in some water filled with salt and chilly.

They used a jack hammer and broke every single bone in his body starting from the ankles, the knees, spine, wrist, elbow and shoulder everything which would be beyond repair and nothing in the world or money could save him to walk again or even to stand properly.

They used an adjustable wrench and pulled out his tongue and cut it in half and made him drink some acid, which destroyed his vocal chords permanently and they poured some acid onto his face and a ruggedly handsome and cruel Leonardo was the ugliest and covered in blood at that point of time.

As the anger was not subsiding, Ambra took out a knife and was about to cut his throat, Amy held her hand and said No, he needs to live. See the world with one eye and can crawl for the rest of his life. His legs and his hands are now not usable and nobody is going to recognize him either.

They removed that wooden plank from under his feet and removed that nail from his heel. They dragged him to the lake nearby, where Brandon and Kevin were talking with each other. They looked at Leonardo and said we haven't tortured anybody like this before. This is total cruelty.

No, said Amy, this is not being cruel, this is making peace with your past, and that's what I like to call it. And we are not going to kill him, we are now going to give him a shower and then dress up all the wounds, so that it will heal in matter of days and he will live. Live until he could see it all. None of his associates are going to recognize him, even if they did, he cannot talk, he cannot even point his fingers, can't walk, he will crawl for the rest of his life in this earth.

This is the least that we could do for a loving brother and for a caring father. And all the Gods above know that what we did is right, we just gave him the judgment that the Gods made and we were born just to complete that mission.

He will definitely see another day but not in the same way.

Brandon and Kevin were still in a state of shock, until the gals shook them off and said its time for us to leave now and there is no point in staying here.

Now, before we proceed, we need to make sure that we are not followed anymore. So next stop Royal Gateways Coffee Shop.

As soon as they were there, Brandon signaled the rest and took off from the car to the nearest CCTV camera with a placard. It read, Leonardo, you coward, the time that you promised that you would be here has passed. And I guess you are not man enough to face the challenge.

Leonardo's tech team saw this and passed the message to all his associates.

Brandon came back to his car, opened his laptop and searched for recent messages from all the phones and it read "Leonardo not with Brandon, come back to base".

And there were a few those who even joked about the situation by saying, he would be still thinking of a way to get better of Brandon. And they had a good laugh about it.

And now that loose end has been taken care of; now off to the place where Kevin left off without a hassle and without anybody on our trail. Looking for what led Franco all the way here and what made him gave up his life.

Ambra said finally, we hunted him down and gave him what he deserved for a vicious animal that he is.

63

All the four of them were out in an open coffee shop not far from the place that they are supposed to go. They were having a hearty laugh and then suddenly Ambra stopped laughing stood up and walked towards the road and she was sipping her coffee looking at the highway and as the tears rolled down her beautiful cheeks, Kevin walked towards her and handed over a tissue with which she could wipe the tears off.

She looked at him, smiled and said – this tissue could wipe the tears over my cheeks, but this is not going to repair the empty space in my heart that my father left, the love and the caring that I used to get from him and this cannot wipe the tears that are rolling down my heart.

Kevin took Ambra and gave her a hug and said I won't be able to give your father back and I won't be able to fill the gap like he used to, but I can promise you this, I can understand every single word that is unspoken and care for you, but that gap that you currently have in you cannot be filled with any of this, but that gap can be sealed with love and tenderness that I can offer and a better life.

She smiled!

But beware, I may be outspoken at times, I will be drunk like a skunk and almost all the times, I'm like a kid whose innocence is beyond imagination and I may be very hard to be with.

Ambra smirked and said I can live with that.

Brandon and Amy were listening to this from a distance; they rose from their seats and walked towards the new romantic couple.

We can drop this here and go back home and have a different life, Brandon said.

No! I wanted to see what brought my father here and I wanted to know what he saw that was so unbelievable. I wanted to know, why we were being chased and was brought to the brim of death. I wanted to see what he left for me...

And she corrected herself.. left for us..

We will stop when I know what it is and what I can do with it. Whatever we might find, we all will take it home. It's ours and not for anyone else.

I would appreciate if you could please be with me on this one and we can have fun in finding this. She pointed on both the directions of the highway and said look now, nobody is following us and we are at our own pace now, please let's not stop here, we can do this together and without you guys, I cannot do this alone. Don't leave me now.

She looked at Kevin and nodded her head asking for his concurrence.

Brandon understood and looked and Kevin and gave him a sign through sign language, it said "Your wish" and he smiled.

Amy understood what they all seek. She took Brandon's hand and walked towards Ambra and Kevin, she took all their hands and raised it, together, we will and we can.

They all took their glasses and said cheers! Amy said "To Us" and all of them unanimously said "To Us"

64

Back in their room, Brandon said it's time for us to revisit the map and its contents. Let's start from the very beginning.

This is what we have currently

1. Look for Rose
2. Beneath the stars
3. The Thickest Tree
4. Pull in Phrygia

I remember Franco has named the file as Treasure Map in his computer. But now I'm not sure where this would lead us. Kevin has found out the area where Franco went, he scanned and took a lot of pictures but none of them were any use to us.

In order for us to have a starting point, we need to have something solid in our hand, like a major clue that could lead or provide us with a starting point.

Ambra rose from the seat with a jerk, the letter.

Letter? Brandon inquired.

The letter that my dad had sent to me from Turkey, just like the one he has sent to you. Do you have it handy, what does the letter say?

"Starting with 32119, as you remember, down the bushes, into the cave, round about 2nd tunnel, 40 feet deep, beware of the rocks and you need to see it to believe it"

'I may not be alive or would have absconded and would be in a situation that I cannot contact you, if you are reading this letter, because certain truths are supposed to be hidden, while certain others are supposed to be destroyed, I shouldn't have left you alone to start this journey, but you are going to finish it for me.

Trust no one – as I said a man would contact you, but I don't know how, he will give you our family code and you can trust only him"

There which means, we need to climb the hill in Phrygia. Hopefully ladies, we sure do hope that you enjoy trekking. We have something to find on top of that hill. And I'm sure the place is well guarded by ancient booby traps. We need to be careful. Franco was able to understand and avoid every single one of them inside, which means, the ideology would be easy for us to understand and deactivate the traps or it would take us days to proceed once we find the place, either ways, we are going to do this without a question.

Yes! We are and we should expect the least expected to be there from poisonous snakes to other rattlers and many more surprises are waiting for us inside or even like the Indiana Jones, there would be a stone and we would have to guess the exact weight and put it there, else the blades or the rocks are going to kill us.

Phew! So let's pack our trekking gear, anti-venom and other requirements before we start in the morning.

Ladies, make sure you have a comfortable outfit as this might be a little tiring and a little out exhausting. Are you ready, Kevin asked?

Yes! We are – Let's dash.

Next day morning, they were beneath the hill of Phrygia and they looked at that magnificent beast in enthusiasm and the ladies left out a sigh, too big, do you think we would be able to cover this in a day?

Brandon smiled and replied, if we can't, we would have to sleep on a rope and we will never know what will happen if we take out eyes or hands off, what Leonardo couldn't this jungle would. And remember, whatever happens do not take your hands off the rope, at least hand should be maintained on the rope at all times.

This is a jungle and after some time, you might feel exhausted and want to rest, call it in, so that all of us would wait, there is no I in a team, only we, but that doesn't mean that you can call it in at any given point of time. We must reach the top before the sun goes to sleep and then we will tent ourselves on top of this.

Not many knows this mountain as Phrygia, this has been mentioned in a lot of books in different names. But with all that is said I personally like this name and we have ~4000+ that we need to climb by evening. A hard task, but we can, less breaks and faster hands makes it a lot easier. Well, as a matter of fact, it is easier said than done. But we need to try and on the way up, we will also check for alternatives that can take us to the top at the earliest.

Brandon took out a gun, it looked like a laser weapon, then pointed it up and shot was fired, a red light came through it and he said there is a landing ground 150 feet above, probably that might help us to get higher easier.

They all pulled out their ear phones and have been connected to any kind of communication. The first 150 feet is going to be the toughest, post that we can have alternatives and can take us to the top very fast.

How is that possible? Inquired Amy, he smiled and said by trusting me.

No, seriously.

Elementary my dear Watson! We can do something from there. Let's see what we can do, as I see a landing ground there, we can use some of our toys there, which we can't from here. I don't want others to see that we have used certain toys from here. And we will even take this rope as we climb up.

This is not trekking, this is close to mountaineering.

Let's face it, we can spend the whole day debating how difficult that this is going to be or we can take the first step and start walking. Think 150 in mind and let's walk.

Well, No pain, no gain and they started to walk.

After a good long walk, they reached the ground, which Brandon saw from beneath. Not too big, but big enough to unload their toys.

He opened the bag and kept small rocket launchers on the ground, he tried a metal string on that and tied the other end onto a false hook that Kevin placed and they fired the rocket launchers, along with the string, the rockets went up and it hit in a place and stopped,

Brandon used his tablet to record it, it has landed close to 2000 feet above.

They tried a hook onto their waist and they pulled in another hook to lock it with the string that was attached to the rocket launchers and once all of them were hooked, he pressed a button and just like a pulley, the string pulled them up slowly.

On the way up, Brandon and Kevin were getting ready with another set of rocket launchers and they fired that just before they hit the spot where the first string was coming to an end, as soon as they reached on top, he removed that hook and hooked it again with the new string that took them to the top of the mountain.

They were excited to be on top, Kevin and Brandon instructed Ambra and Amy to open the box and to fix the tent, while they cleared the area to place the tent and went hunting to get them something to eat.

They reached on top around 8:00PM, which was a long journey, they were tired and exhausted. I don't think none of us have any stamina, as I feel Franco did all this and went back to his hotel in less than 20 hours and we took close to 9 hours to climb up all the way up and we are already exhausted.

Amy pulled out her air bed and said I'm going to bed and I don't want to think what's in store for us tomorrow, while they all looked at each other.

65

Brandon had a campfire set up and he was heating up his marsh mellows, he missed them and he missed his days like these in the force. They knew what they were supposed to do when the day breaks and but didn't know what to anticipate in front of them and that made the days more thrilling and adventurous. But there were also days, when their spies would tell them what's in store for them, but again, when you know your future, the future has already changed. You go with the flow and that makes it more interesting.

Amy couldn't sleep much, she had her winter throw on and she came out of the tent and saw Brandon sitting there along with his marsh mellows. She joined him and sat really close to him. If I have to read you Brandon, you are still a virgin married to your force and dreams and you've lived like that long enough to see the difference.

Don't underestimate me, I can be really bad, but as a matter of fact, nobody has read me so perfectly like you, but you know what, that is a fact, I haven't had any desire, my job was my life but today, I do sometimes regret that decision.

Have you ever given it a thought about a woman coming into your life now?

I have, but I'm not sure, how I would be able to actually take it, you know, I have been doing everything on my own and I'm so used to it, there were a lot of things that actually held me back, my enemies, there are a lot of them, if they knew that I'm still alive, might not sleep until they put a bullet right here, while he tapped his temple.

Sometimes, life is strange, it never gives you what you want, but it will show the opportunity that leads to the door that has what you want, but we would be so prejudice that we won't even see that door.

Yeah! You are right, but understand this, life gives you more than one similar opportunity to give you what you want and only a real fool would slide it away all the time. And it's not because of our prejudice mind that we miss that opportunity, it is mostly because we are scared to open that door to find ourselves out of the comfort zone and as we don't know what's really hiding behind that door.

Amy smiled at his statement. But you should understand, some doors are really good, you should open it sometimes and you would be amazed to see what you find in there.

Brandon smiled and said I would love to open one door and I'm sure, that I would be amazed, because today at this very moment, I'm having a feeling that is going to be one hell a journey along with a likeminded person, who understands and cares.

Amy understood what he meant, but her face didn't show.

Brandon leaned over and with a smile Amy did too for that kiss that she always long for; a kiss with care, understanding and loyalty. It felt like all her troubles and pain just went by.

Oh! Brandon, I don't want to lose you ever.

You should understand one thing Amy, living with me would be the most difficult thing that you would have done. No knowledge about the outside world, a man who has been used to getting things done all alone, no dependency and no next to kin on record. You will never know what will happen to me in days to come, will I be revealed, it can be anything, I cannot promise you a happy ending and I cannot promise you the sky, the only thing that I can promise you at this given point of time is total security and I'm not as romantic I may seem, I can be very harsh and hard sometimes.

I can live with that. In these few days, I have noticed, you are a good listener and you care and I wish all the men are like that, but alas! None of them are like that. It's very hard to get such a combination of a listener and a person who cares; to me rest all is immaterial. And she got up to hit the bed.

Brandon smiled and lied down looking at the stars.

66

The day broke and all of them slept peacefully than ever.

The time was around 11:30AM, by the time they all were up from their beds. That was a good sleep all of the commented, peaceful and free. It's been sometime since I've slept like a baby commented Brandon and he smiled. But this, definitely feels good, it just shows how tired we all were from all the recent episodes in our lives.

In a distance, not far away, Ambra saw a shimmering light and that made Brandon and Kevin to look in the same direction, while Amy was busy making them a coffee over the last night's campfire.

That looks like a piece of metal. They all dressed up real quick, forget the coffee; they all buckled their shoes and started walking in the direction of the light.

It looks like a piece of metal, remarked Brandon from a distance.

As they neared that object, Ambra ran towards that and picked it up in her hand and said it's my father's lucky charm, he always carries this around for luck; I guess he left it here to show us where he was and to tell me something else. They looked around the place and couldn't find anything out of the ordinary.

Regular trees, the leaves on the ground, dusty and nothing stood out of the usual. Brandon said usually, we would find some clue if there is a way, but not really sure. I don't see anything. Even it can be the wild winds that brought this charm here, he might have kept it safe somewhere else, we might never know.

I don't think so said Ambra, if he wanted us to know the place that we need to look for, he would keep it there and he wouldn't be so hasty in leaving something that is so precious to him like this.

She has got a point, said Kevin.

And a point well taken, said Brandon; Amy looked around to find anything that could tie this thing together, but was in vain.

Kevin took the compass from his pocket and remembered the star that was in the map, right in the middle of the paper.

Please get me the map, I want to look into something, guys, remember this star, we all were looking for this meaning, which we were not able to decipher initially, I have a clue may or may not work. But it's worth a try. What is it?

We found this piece of charm here, so we take four steps ahead and three steps left.

Ok, what did you find asked Brandon?

Nothing, said Kevin, I'm still here and there is nothing around me.

Brandon said let me look at this.

He looked at the charm; it looked like a star, but of course completely out of shape. But then, he looked at the tree where he found the charm, he slowly moved from finger from top and moved down slowly, until, he found a crack, which almost looked like it was pointing to an object, but again that was a mere speculation, there he saw a bunch of stones laid in order one over the other to form a statue. A statue that looked like Merlin Monroe in her early teens, he commented and they just laughed about it, right in the middle of a jungle, where it would have taken days without proper gear to climb all the way up in those years.

They proceeded to the statue slowly from head down, all around he observed and there were inscriptions on certain stones, he used tooth brush and water to clean those rocks to have a better look, it was nothing, it was just a shape of a pentacle and there were only five with pentacle inscription on, he took a photograph of that statue and instructed everyone not to touch it.

He immediately pulled his gear out and his laptop along with his foldable and a portable printer that he carries along. He loaded that photograph onto his system, enlarged it and took a printout of that picture immediately.

He joined the all the pentacles using a marker that he had and that was another pentacle. And all of them were baffled. This is a puzzle and I know none other than Franco, who is good at cracking these kinds of things, but unfortunately he is not here with us and we need to break this before we could proceed.

Kevin said you made this discovery so much, cracked the original map, cracked this so much and this one in record time, so we believe in you and I'm sure you would be able to crack this one as well. He smiled.

Brandon nodded his head in disagreement.

Kevin and Ambra started walking slowly out to nowhere, while Amy stood beside Brandon to give him a helping hand. He sat on the floor with his laptop and all his widgets came into play. Amy was going through what he was looking for and then, Amy looked at the map and the pentacle that he drew.

But nothing stuck out, they both scratched their heads with different possibilities, but was not confident enough to try because, this can be a trap as well, if the incorrect ones are pressed, there is a chance that this entire thing will get locked out and there would be no way that they could open this, until and unless they find the secret door out of the treasure chamber that would be an easy one, but they cannot find it without proper papers and nobody draws about that in any paper.

After some time, they started to feel tired, exhausted and out of breath, sitting in the hot sun for hours while the brain is at work, they were about to get a sunstroke and that's the time when Kevin and Ambra turned up with a bottle of water and something to munch on.

They were so relieved and Brandon took a bottle of water and poured it all over his head, which gave him the strength to proceed. They were slowly getting hungrier by the minute and something to munch and water was not giving them what they wanted.

Kevin and Ambra came back with some bread toasts and bacon, which they were supposed to have for breakfast; they cleared their plates in less time than it took for them to open the contents of the packets to cook.

Kevin and Ambra started to continue their walk and didn't want to disturb the duo as they were breaking their heads to come up with an idea.

Amy looked at the picture and the map and told Brandon, may be.....just a may be, what if this pentacle and tapped the one on the top with their index finger, come down four stones, take a left and count three stones, you will reach this pentacle, this second one at the bottom, that is the only logical explanation that I can give at this point of time looking at this map and the drawing that you made.

Brandon couldn't believe his ears and he instantly kissed Amy, you have your moments too. She smiled and he could see her pride in her eyes.

It's worth a try, let's do it.

What about them? If it is right, we will call them, else, let's get back to work.

As you said Brandon pressed the first stone on the top, he could hear a cracking sound and this made Kevin and Ambra run back to the spot and join with Amy and Brandon.

Brandon looked tensed, this could either lock or open the door that we are looking for and I have no idea what is going to pop out or what is waiting for us. Let's see where it leads us.

He pressed the stone in, the second at the bottom, he could hear another cracking sound and the tree and had Franco's lucky charm moved and there stood a tunnel, a tunnel that can fit one person at a time beneath it.

They stood there looking inside that tunnel, with their flashlights and Brandon threw one of the flash lights into the tunnel.

A few seconds later, the tree started to move again and this time, the tree closed the tunnel and the stones in the statue popped back out, ready to be pressed again.

67

Now is the best part that is going to happen, I'm going to press those stones again and we are going to jump, there are chances that we might get separated inside, but I don't think we need to take that chance, so we tie us together with a this and then we jump, we will naturally follow the one in the front and we all will come together, the only problem would be, small bruises and there, when the person who is leading us takes a diversion or make sudden changes.

That's ok, as long as we are together said Amy.

Now before that, we need to read that letter that Franco wrote to Ambra after visiting this place.

I think, this is in reverse order, I think he made sure that he doesn't give them straight answers in case this letter finds its way into the wrong hands.

So it's like this, this tunnel is going to be 40 feet deep and we are going to land on the rocks, then we proceed through the bushes and then we take a roundabout and take the 2ⁿᵈ tunnel and get into a cave. I think, that's what it says, but the only way to find that out is we jump and if we land on the rocks we would know. Before that, he took out his recorder, read the letter and what it was on the map and kept it on his phone, just in case, rather than reading it all the time.

Brandon went ahead to push the stones on the status again, while others started to tie themselves up in the waist and kept a piece at the end for Brandon to tie himself. As he came back after pressing those stones, he said we would jump and this is not going to be the way out, we need to find that too.

Amy tied Brandon and Kevin asked him to lead. He looked at Ambra, while Ambra nodded in approval.

The tree started to move again and Brandon jumped and so did others along with him, while the tree closed the entrance above them, leaving them in total darkness, until Brandon used his flash light to see where they were going.

----

40 feet depth the tunnel was, the landing was not that great, everybody on top of each other on the rocks, mild bruises here and there, but they were all safe.

Brandon stretched his neck to comfort himself and proceeded towards the only way, that led them through the bushes to a large room with two tunnels in their path on the other side. This is not right said Brandon and signed them to stay there and he came to the middle of that room and looked towards where they were standing to find another two, one they came from and one beside that.

He said take a roundabout and get into the second tunnel and all of them were on their knees, crawling through that tunnel. It was quite a long tunnel, their knees started to pain, they couldn't even stand up and rest, the tunnel was only that big.

After sometime, they came to the end of the tunnel, which directed them to a cave and as they entered the cave, there was a waterfall, right inside the cave and they had no idea where the water was coming from.

They made their way towards the waterfall and went in to find a huge rock blocking their entrance, which they had no idea how to open it.

All of them, sat in different places and were trying to catch their breath after a long crawl and walking through the waterfall.

All of them were ready to give up but not Brandon, he was not a quitter; he was trying to figure out a way to get back on track, while the others being so pessimistic in continuing the journey. While Brandon got angry said Didn't I warn you about the obstacles that we need to face and the hindrances that might have in this journey, if you were not ready for this game, you should have decided that we are not going to do this and we will take a plane back home as soon as our work in Turkey was done. But no, you guys wanted to do this, a thrilling adventure, an experience that you wanted to tell your grand kids or boast about this in some stupid club with whom they have no interest in hearing other than giving their complete attention to what's happening in rest of the world through the big TV screens and want to sip that good old scotch in their hands and brag about the money that they made in the stock market with the help of the government who actually made the world believe that they lost billions along with the major banks in the world who gave them a helping hand to do so and in the long run the rich got richer while the poor got poorer.

And I don't know if you have noticed, there is no way out of here other than the door that would lead us to the outside world and that door would be located inside where all the treasures are kept and let me tell you again, **IF** there is a treasure.

All of them were quiet, as they haven't seen Brandon like this before, he can always cool and composed. Kevin said he has all the right to be upset, he is the one who cracked everything down and we were just going behind and doing things that were instructed, we haven't used our brains at all, while he did and he had spent a lot of sleepless nights looking after us and Yes! He did warn us to and it is us who wanted to proceed with this journey.

We are not quitters, so lets get involved and try to give Brandon a helping hand.

Brandon took a deep breath and said – Thank You!

68

Brandon, along with others started to look for clues, clues that were hidden in those walls. Amy knew how Brandon worked, have worked with him once and that gave Amy a clear picture how he worked and he tried to relate to things. Brandon took his laptop from his bag, that's when Amy realized, how serious he is with all these matters, he even thought about the smallest detail, like having a waterproof bag to go with.

Brandon took out his camera and laptop as usual, but this time, he was not able to get the kind of images he would like to work with, due to lack of light inside that cave, but he knew there had to be something that would lead him there basically with only a flashlight at his disposal.

It took him hours to notice a pentacle on top of the cave, then he tried to correlate it with the map again, he tried searching for the other pentacles on that wall. Amy suddenly noticed how Brandon's flashlight was moving on those walls and she knew what exactly he was looking for.

She also tried to help him by having her flashlight moving the same paths and that's when Brandon realized that she is the one for him, that she is able to hear his unspoken words and his thoughts, he smiled at her and moved forward until he located all the other pentacles that were on that wall.

He called everyone, Ambra and Kevin were tired looking for something that they didn't even knew. Brandon said I think I know how to open this door, but again, I don't know how long that is going to hold of how long will stay open. So as soon as the door opens make sure that you walk in.

They all nodded, Brandon found a stone that would be appropriate to use. He aimed for the top pentacle and threw the stone. Everybody watched that in absolute shock, that was an astounding throw.

Direct hit, bull's eye. The first stone was pushed. Brandon then walked towards the cave and pressed the second last one and waited in anticipation. Nothing happened. He bent his head down in disappointment. He nodded his head, this can't be right. That's when his eyes fall on a carving of a rose beneath all the stars. He inspected that rose, it was carved well in stone, not that easy to find. He looked up and he saw a small opening through which, he could see the sky in a distance. He remembered "Look for the Rose" "Beneath the stars"; he couldn't relate it whether they talked about the sky of the carvings on the wall. Anyways, he started looking frantically in all direction, but not a tree in sight. But in corner between two walls, he saw a wooden plank camouflaged as a stone. He slowly moved ahead in that direction. Watched closely and observed the plank "The thickest tree" and that wooden plank was the closest that he could relate it to, "Pull in Phrygia" and using a crowbar he pulled it. And they could hear a sound of a door getting opened on the side of the cave, the door he thought would open didn't but another one did.

All rushed to that door and walked in before that one closed. Just as they anticipated, the door closed behind them.

It was dark and it was dusty, even the flashlights were running out of battery, they all panicked and didn't know what can be done.

Brandon noticed a fire torch on the wall, he used his zippo and lit one of those and there were a hundred's of them side by side all over the wall from one torch to the other, the fire carried on, until the entire room was filled with light and they were able to see what was inside that cave.

Hundreds of scrolls from the period of the kings and the queens. Statues made from Ruby and Sapphire, the size of the rooms was about the size of two Trafalgar square put together. What was that Franco wanted us to see, he could have just given Leonardo what he wanted, but why didn't do that, a question that ran through Brandon's head from the time he set his eyes on the treasure. Franco is not the kind of person who would let himself killed for this piece of treasure, he didn't say that aloud, but a question he was asking himself.

They walked the entire length up and down looking at all the treasures that they could find. Brandon was busy looking for a way out and he found one right at the end of the room, stairs to climb and walk out without any hassle.

But the question kept haunting him.

Until he bumped into a statue of gold. A statue that looked like an 8 year old, the bigger version of which he saw outside carved in different stone. He didn't understand the significance. Franco knew the significance of that statue, that is the reason why he didn't want to give the location of this to another person. Two statues, same thing. The one outside is slightly bigger and would look like a 20 year old lady, but this one is much younger more like an 8 year old or less.

That is when, he recollected the wording of the letter that Franco had sent to Ambra, *"You my child is made of Gold"* initially he thought, Franco was referring to Ambra, but when he saw this statue, he knew it was not able Ambra, Franco was talking about this statue.

What's the significance of this statue, of the statue carved in stone outside and the letter, there has to be a connection. The statue outside is for people to know, they have arrived at the right spot to uncover the truth about this statue made of Gold. Letter and the statue, I think I saw, someones child – statue of Gold.

Oh! My God!

Is it even possible, he thought loudly.

What happened? All of them inquired.

Brandon pointed his index finger towards that statue and asked them what do you think??

Nothing, just a statue made of gold.

NO!

You don't see any significance in this statue, the one above carved in stone and the letter from Franco wrote to Ambra – *"You my child is made of gold"*

They said we don't see any significance.

Seriously guys, you need to use your brain sometimes before it rusts completely..

Let me give you a clue.. Brandon talked about what he thinks about the statue above and this one. They nodded in agreement. Now about the letter, whose child is actually made of Gold?

Amy said No way…

Yes! It is true, this is his daughter, who once walked on this earth in flesh and blood..

Yes! Said Brandon This is King Midas's daughter, which means the legend is true, while the trio stood there shell shocked.

EPILOGUE

One year later...

Good Morning sweet heart.. as Amy pulled the blanket over Brandon's face.

Brandon opened his eyes and said Good Morning.

Do you remember what day it is today? Yes! I do, our third wedding anniversary.

Oh! Baby you remember,

I do, I also remember three years before, we got married a week later we found that treasure. We were not total losers, we just took a few valuables, left his daughter there and listened to what our dear friend had said certain things are better hidden and some are worth destruction.

Yes! We kept that hidden, from everyone, even if there is a copy of this map exists, they can't get there, because, we destroyed the stone structure that was there on that mountain as some treasures are too big for one man to handle sometimes even the king.

Around lunch time, Amy's phone rings...

Hello!

Wishing you a very happy and prosperous wedding day!

Thank you Ambra... How are you doing?

Great.. Thank you.

How about Kevin?

He is doing good too..and they have a laugh.

What's he doing?

He is planning to move the lawn for the past one week... he is currently cuddled up on his lazy boy and is watching a game with a beer and I'm going to switch that off and throw him out, so that the lawn could be moved at least today.

They talk about their husbands and laugh for some time and then Amy says, you know what Ambra, we all should get together sometime

That's when Kevin and Brandon came to the phone and shouted.... We all should.....

Hari Menon who lives in India with his wife and twins. He has been working in the corporate world for more than a decade and has published a lot of articles and poetries in wide range of arrays. Travelling being one of his interest, he tries to be as creative as he can be in brining the life that we experiences first hand into his writing.

You can reach the author at
Email: hkmenon@outlook.com
Facebook: www.facebook.com/authorhk